The Morningstar Confession

Matthew Lutton

THE MORNINGSTAR CONFESSION

MATTHEW LUTTON

Copyright © 2024 by Matthew Lutton

All rights reserved.

No part of this publication may be reproduced, distributed, or transmitted in any form or by any means, including photocopying, recording, or other electronic or mechanical methods without the prior written permission of the publisher, except as permitted by U.S. copyright law. For permission requests, contact zurenarrh44 @gmail.com

The story, all names, characters, and incidents portrayed in this production are fictitious. No identification with actual persons (living or deceased), places, buildings, and products is intended or should be inferred.

Paperback ISBN: 979-8-9910633-3-3

Cover Artist: Marcelle Silva

Editor: Jyl Glenn

Interior Formatting: Jyl Glenn

First edition 2024

For Lisa,

Thank you for your faith in me
and the push to do this.

Contents

Author's Note	1
Epigraph	3
Chapter 1 In the Beginning	4
Chapter 2 Who Cannot Grow a Feather	20
Chapter 3 Groveling in the Dust	31
Chapter 4 Crawl	37
Chapter 5 Truth or Gospel	49
Chapter 6 A Goodly Apple	71
Chapter 7 The Darkness Now Seems Normal	102
Chapter 8 The Truth is Not in Us	163

Chapter 9 The Greatest Trick	191
Patreon Thanks	207
Also by Matt Lutton	208
About the author	209

Author's Note

I started writing this book a year ago, but in truth, I've been writing it my whole life. Religion is a tough topic—one that can cost friendships—but since you bought the book—I feel it's worth addressing here. I believe in God, though we don't always see eye to eye. This has been a lifelong struggle. As a kid, God was like Santa—always watching over me. But as I grew up, I began to question if He was watching at all. Despite a privileged upbringing, my faith wavered, as the world can be cruel, and it's natural to wonder where God is in tough times.

At 13, I started asking questions. I attended different churches, read religious texts, and sought out religious speakers. Some of the stories were beautiful, others disturbing. So I asked the hard questions, and often left disappointed. The blame for my doubt was frequently placed on one figure—Lucifer. I knew him as the Devil, but I became curious about his story. After reading everything I could find on him, I began to empathize with him. Perhaps it was my rebellious nature or being a middle child, but I understood why he wouldn't bow to humans. He too, wasn't seen.

This book is about that—feeling unseen and the impact it can have, even on someone like the Lightbringer.

My hope is that this book makes you think, entertains you, and encourages you to see the people in your life. It's not a religious text, nor an attack on faith. It's about finding faith in myself. I never thought I could write more than short stories, but someone believed in me and pushed me to tell this story.

If you haven't read Lamb by Christopher Moore, I recommend it. I pay homage to it through my use of the name Joshua.

Thank you to everyone who's supported me. Your belief in my stories keeps me going.

Enjoy.

-Matt Lutton
　Marysville, WA
　　September 2024

"But who prays for Satan? Who, in eighteen centuries, has had the common humanity to pray for the one sinner that needed it most?"

—Mark Twain

Chapter 1
In the Beginning

The night was warm and humid as of late and Dan hated it almost as much as he hated listening to the same old sins over and over. Each night it was more of the same thing. Adultery was, of course, the biggest one, but he guessed with there being only seven and all, his choice of nightly sin variety was pretty slim. This usually gave him a chuckle and made him brush off his vestments, tuck the cigarette which he fought to not light daily back into its cylindrical tube. Then he would perform the sign of the cross as he walked back into his church to listen to anyone who might need confession. That is what usually happened, but tonight was different. The humidity had a vacuum effect. It was almost like the atmosphere was reclaiming the oxygen from his lungs that he had stolen from it ever since he was born.

His collar was tight, his robes seemed more like a straitjacket than a vestment. So, to get some form of relief, he loosened his cloth and anointed his neck and forehead with the holy water, which probably should have been refreshed a couple of nights ago. *The Lord protects against all things except stagnant, smelly water,* Dan thought, breathing a little easier as the cool liquid calmed him.

Looking around at the church, he felt a sense of pride mixed with the coolness and his worry dissipated. He had turned what was once a long-forgotten building into what could be a shining beacon of light to his community. It had taken hard work and all the money he had, as little as that might have been, to grow it into the little congregation of about forty he would welcome on Sundays. He was no mega church, but he was not a Pentecostal either, and that suited him fine.

The red light blinked on above the confessional. Dan wiped himself dry as he made his way into the little box he had inherited from a decommissioned church a couple of states over. The wood creaked under the pressure of his weight, and he smiled to himself, thinking the noise gave the old gal some character and a personality. Dan needed to get out more, otherwise he would be naming the furniture soon, he thought as he pulled the divider open.

The smell of cinnamon and fresh apples flowed through the air. A welcome change from the usual sweat and cheap perfume that most men covered themselves in, seeking forgiveness only a short drive from where they had performed the act itself. It usually took two cans of Febreze to get the odor out of the little box.

"Are these things always so uncomfortable?" the voice on the other side of the partition sounded genuinely curious.

"I'm sorry, my son. Do you have a confession?" Dan asked, ignoring the question and the slight offense he felt from it.

"I mean, I guess it makes sense. You Catholics love punishing yourselves," the voice replied with a chuckle.

Dan sat closer to the screen, which separated him and the stranger.

"You are not Catholic?"

"Well...come to think of it, I guess I am. I mean, I have been baptized."

"Have you taken Holy communion?" Dan asked, checking off the list.

"It's been ages, but I have indeed."

"Then you are a Catholic. Congratulations." He thought himself clever, with little jokes like this amongst his congregation.

"So, what troubles you, my son?" He leaned back into his cushion.

"How much time you got, padre?" The man laughed, letting the question linger.

Dan smiled to himself. He knew what it was like to not see the world the way it should be.

"Let's start with what brought you in tonight, shall we?"

"Humans." It was simple and to the point.

"I've never heard it put like that, but what is it about humanity that troubles you so?"

"The pride mainly. I think."

"That is the root of all sins."

"So, I've been told."

Dan chuckled and waited for the stranger to continue, but all he heard was silence.

"Do go on," Dan insisted.

"I don't feel better," the voice said gravely.

"Why would you? You have not confessed anything, nor have I forgiven you."

"I thought you lot were already forgiven, so why the need to ask for it?"

The question took Dan by surprise.

"We believe it brings us closer to God. It also gives us a better recollection of how to be better." Dan smiled to himself. He liked to think his method of teaching the word was modern and not archaic or boring, like so many other priests.

"I thought only God had the authority to forgive you?"

"This is true; however, Christ deemed his priest mediators on earth."

"I understand now."

Dan nodded, thinking himself quite the teacher.

"You believe yourselves to have equal authority."

"That is correct." Dan's smile grew.

"To God?"

The smile evaporated as he shook his head in protest.

"No! Of course, we are not equal to God. We are merely his mouthpiece and humble servants on earth."

"Jesus then?" the voice asked.

"Jesus what?" Dan asked in confusion.

"Christ," the tone sounding like it should have been obvious.

"I know who Jesus is…" Dan was growing impatient.

"I would hope so. Considering you lot fancy yourselves twins and all."

He didn't like to kick people out of the church, but on occasion, it had to be done. The local homeless would sometimes get too drunk and rowdy, and Dan would have to shuffle them outside. This stranger did not seem homeless, but Dan was considering showing him the exit, anyway.

"I'm afraid I can't help you. Now, I have other matters to attend to."

"Do you all flee when pushed so gently? How did you all find the time to build that palace in Rome, then?" the voice asked sarcastically.

Dan got up to exit the box but found himself feeling very heavy and needing to sit.

"We're not done yet. I still have questions I need answered." The voice sounded different now, almost farther away.

"I told you there is nothing for you here," Dan said, trying to catch his breath.

"I was hungry, and you gave me food, I was thirsty, and you gave me drink, I was a stranger, and you welcomed me."

"So, you know the word. I don't know what you want, however, and therefore, can offer you nothing. You say you have come to confess, so please do otherwise please leave."

"Again, I ask you what the point of the sacrifice was then?" the voice repeated, sounding like it had done so numerous times.

Dan wiped the sweat from his brow, making his sleeve wet and heavy.

"The sacrifice was for all of our sins, but we still sin daily and so to keep close to God we confess," Dan said, hoping that this answer would somehow appease the very heat he felt.

"Sounds like bullshit. Tell me, what do you believe?"

"I'm a priest. It's not my place to question God's will."

"You just said Christ gave you authority to speak for him. So, I'm asking you what the point of a sacrifice was if you need to continue paying for it?"

"It's complicated," Dan said, frustration showing in his voice.

"It sure sounds like it," the voice sighed.

"Confession eases our souls and allows us entry into the kingdom of heaven. Christ did cleanse our sins on the cross, but that does not stop us from sinning daily, and so to stay close to God and to honor that sacrifice we confess our sins."

"See now, that is an argument," the voice said in agreement.

Dan sat back, finally at peace. He had made his case.

"I do need your help, Dan, and I do seek forgiveness."

Dan went right into the script, growing physically exhausted with each new sentence.

"How many days since your last confession?"

"The last time I confessed how I truly felt, I was thrown out of my home," the voice replied with a hint of sadness.

"You need not have any fear of that happening here. You are safe here. This is God's house, and all are welcome," Dan proclaimed.

The box vibrated from the boisterous laughter the stranger was emitting.

"Is something funny?" He knew he shouldn't let the stranger get to him, but he was growing tired of being mocked.

"I don't believe all are welcome, especially me."

"Nothing you have done will make God turn away from you," Dan said, trying to comfort the voice.

"Then why did he? Why cast me out and not forgive me? Why make me the reason for all of your failures?" The voice's tone shifted like it was hurt. It scared Dan.

"My failures?" he whispered. Asking the question of himself as much as to the stranger.

"Do you want to know what bugs me the most? I hated you. When you were first created, he looked at you in ways he never looked at me and I absolutely despised you for it. Then he tells me you're more important. And not only are you more important, but that he loves you more than anything."

Dan nodded to himself, putting his thoughts at ease. This was actually a common occurrence, where a Satanist or Atheist would claim to be God, Jesus, and sometimes even the Devil himself. Believe it or not, over the years he started to welcome these debates and sometimes he dared say, even enjoyed them.

"No one is above God. It is not our place to question his judgment."

"Oh, that rolls off the tongue when you're the one being praised, doesn't it? Let me ask you then, Dan. If Christ proclaimed dogs were now higher than humans, that you all should wait on them hand and foot, granted some of you do already, would you follow that holy decree?"

Dan chuckled. He had indeed allowed animals into the church recently to accommodate people and keep his congregation growing.

"Let us make mankind in our image, in our likeness, so that they may rule over the fish in the sea, and the birds in the sky, over the livestock and all the wild animals, and over all the creatures that move along the ground." Dan let it hang in the air as if the question could not be pressed further.

"So, you are smarter than the beast?"

"Yes."

"You are stronger than the beast through power, either physically or through ingenuity?"

"We are."

"And you are more beautiful to the creator over these beasts, yes?"

"You are starting to paraphrase, but yes, I guess you could say so," Dan leveraged.

"So even the mere question of God asking you to bow before a beast of lower intellect, beauty, and strength is almost laughable to you?"

"I do not laugh at God," he said defensibly.

"Humor me, Dan."

"Yes, I see many of us not understanding that line of thinking, if you will."

"I didn't either." Anger resonated in the statement.

"However..."

"Oh, this should be rich."

"If God decreed animals were to be taken care of above humanity, then I believe the faithful would indeed follow his command."

The laughter erupted again, shaking the very box that held them. Dan gripped the old wooden seat until knuckles were white and held on, quietly praying to himself that an earthquake didn't ruin his precious old building.

"Are you daft? 881 species you lot have decimated since you started writing things down and one would think maybe that would slow you down. But no, you have wiped out almost 20% and that's just the animals you claim you would 'take care of'. You don't even take care of yourselves, for fuck's sake. You lot have killed and tortured each other ever since those two dumb, inbred bastards fought over a sacrifice!" The voice sounded annoyed now, like he had seen where this conversation was headed, and he was disappointed.

"Satan put evil into the world. This is true, but with God's help and prayer, we can fight back against his influence," Dan said, matching the stranger's tone as he too had heard this fight before.

"Influence? For being so evil and less than, you lot sure do give me an awful amount of power over your little actions, don't you? Tell you what, I'll make you a bet. I will stay here and talk with you for exactly one minute." The sound of a watch's second hand echoed throughout the little box.

"How are you doing that?" Dan asked, having to cover his own ears as the clicks became a cacophony bouncing off the little soundproof walls. Dan kicked at the old wood doors, but they wouldn't budge. His knuckles bloodied as he pounded the wood to no avail until finally the sound ceased. Dan opened his mouth over and over, trying to test his hearing, until the voice on the other side startled him.

"We both agree I've been with you this whole minute?" the voice asked like it was conducting an experiment and needed clarification.

"What was that? I need to leave," he said, trying to open the old doors.

"Don't tap out on me now, Dan. We were just getting into a good little rapport. So, sixty seconds, we can both agree on that, yes?" the voice said, knocking on the wood on his side for emphasis.

"What? No, something is wrong..." His voice trailed off as he looked around the little box, the sound becoming louder as he felt more claustrophobic.

Dan's vision went black, and then he felt it all over his body. The warmth of the red liquid that covered his tightly gripped hands. The hard plastic of the knife left an impression on his skin as he thrust the blade of it against the man, whose protest and grip on Dan's own throat weakened with each insertion. Dan tried to stop his hands, but he had no control over his own body and then he realized that his skin was not his own but belonged to a much darker man than him and suddenly Dan was back in the little box with no blood or dead man before him.

"Dear God in heaven, what was that?" His hands trembled as he wiped his eyes, hoping to wake up in bed with this all being some nightmare.

"That was a murder that occurred in South Africa during the minute we have been talking. There is a murder every sixty seconds on this planet, Dan. And I, as powerful as I am, cannot be responsible for every one of those, now can I?"

He wasn't listening. His thoughts were trying to explain the images he had seen, the sensations he had felt.

"The wine, maybe? Too much wine," Dan said.

"You don't drink that much," the voice retorted.

"Weed. Could it have been that?" Dan looked through the tiny holes in desperation.

"From when you were in high school? C'mon man, I know you're not exactly a man of science, but that's not how that works," the voice chuckled.

"Who are you? What have you done to me?" Dan demanded.

"I have a lot of names, Dan."

"I want you out of my church and I want out of this box," he demanded

"Oh, now it's your church. I thought this was God's house?"

He was pounding on the little wooden door now, screaming for help.

"Dan...DAN, please, nobody is coming," the voice stated.

He stopped hitting the door and slumped down in defeat.

"What do you want from me?" he pleaded.

"I told you, I want you to confess."

"You're forgiven. Now please go," Dan said with some hope.

"We both know that's not how it works, so don't insult me." The voice sounded annoyed.

Dan didn't understand what was happening, but he realized he was this man's hostage now and the best course of action was to play along.

"Tell me your sins then, dammit!" He just wanted this nightmare to be over.

"It's just one."

"Perfect, then let's hear it." Dan tried to slow his breathing at the thought this might be at an end sooner rather than later.

"I need to tell you the whole thing for it to make sense."

"Of course you do," Dan said through gritted teeth, rubbing his hands over his knees in frantic strokes. He counted down from five, breathing in and out, until his voice was steady enough to sound somewhat professional. He took in one last breath and let it out, finishing it with the sign of the cross.

"You're saying you're the actual devil?" Dan was making sure he had heard correctly.

"This all goes a lot easier if you just take my word for it."

The voice said it like he had been through this many times.

"Let's say for argument's sake that I believe you. Will you let me go after I hear your confession?"

"I give you my word."

Dan chuckled to himself; the irony not lost on him with the Devil giving his word.

"I don't need to sign anything? No pact for my soul?" he said mockingly.

"I don't do deals. I have others working in that department."

"Of course, of course. May I ask, though, why souls? What do you do with them, exactly?"

"I'll let you in on a secret, Dan. One I've never told anyone, not even my second in command."

Dan laughed at himself as he caught himself inching closer to the partition with curiosity.

"Go on," he said, trying to not sound too eager.

"Not...a...damn...thing."

"I've never heard that one before," Dan chuckled.

"No, and why would you? We've never met before tonight."

"I mean, what's the point of collecting souls if you're not going to do anything with them?" The question was out of genuine curiosity.

"They are important to Him because they are important to you and thus..."

Dan was nodding.

"So, you collect them to spite God," he concluded.

"Most things you humans do are to spite him as well, from the look of it," the voice retorted.

Dan found himself nodding again.

"It's true. It is tough to see all the misery in the world and not think we have turned away from God and his plan, but I have faith, and as long as there is faith, there is hope." He smiled to himself.

"Bullshit."

Dan's smile dissipated. "What?"

"It's bullshit! You haven't turned away from God, you're just doing what comes naturally. It's unfair, the pressure you lot put on yourselves, honestly." The voice sounded almost sympathetic.

"You think rape, murder, and general cruelty are human nature?" He was offended by the idea.

"I don't think anything, I'm certain of it! I was there when he made you out of clay."

"That's a little bit of a cop-out, wouldn't you say? 'I was there.' So, I'm just supposed to take your word for it?" The sarcasm dripped from his words.

"Call it faith, Dan." The voice replied in a sly tone.

"Tell me how you fell then, oh, great dragon." He was enjoying this a little too much.

"I don't enjoy being mocked." The statement was a warning.

Dan cleared his throat and spoke sincerely. "I'm sorry. I lost myself for a moment."

"Not a problem."

"Thank you, my son."

"It's in your nature, after all."

Dan chuckled and breathed in deep.

"Alright, please tell me how you fell."

"That always made me laugh. Fell!? Like I tripped and stumbled off a cloud into the abyss? I didn't fall, Dan, I was pushed."

Chapter 2
Who Cannot Grow a Feather

The light was beautiful. It always made him feel like he had accomplished something, even when he had only opened his eyes. Angels did not need sleep, but Lucifer enjoyed the darkness at times, especially when the moon was shining down on the earth. It illuminated the world in a different tone and invited God's creatures to hunt instead of the beasts who ruled in the daylight. Birds were his favorite; he often would outstretch his wings and compare his own to the hunter's as he admired it swooping through the air and clutching a mouse in its talons.

He enjoyed watching the mice as well. They were interesting creatures who would scurry about collecting scraps and invading the dens of insects. The breeding process astounded Lucifer. One bitch could produce six pups every couple cycles of light. They were lucky they bred so bountifully because the mice were greedy things, throwing logic and caution aside to dart across the field, knowing the owl was up on high. Almost daring it to catch them, and it often did. One moment in particular had been haunting Lucifer's memory as of late. An old tree had recently been broken by a storm and some field mice had made it their home. The two mice decorated it and brought in leaves to make it warm. Until one night, an owl decided he would be making this tree his home.

The owl was old and not expecting much more than chasing one of the former tenants through the field, but as his beak crushed the skull of one mouse, the other dodged and hissed inside the hollow. This, by itself, was nothing to be excited about, as any creature backed into a corner will fight for its life. But the mouse was outmatched and had a clear exit while the Owl feasted on its unlucky mate. The mouse made the decision to stay and stood its ground. Tiny teeth bit at the old owl's leathery feet, making it screech and spread its wings, constricted by the wall of the tiny hollow. The owl pecked and slashed, but for being so wise, it kept flapping its wings like a dragon. It was too big for its own cave and trapped itself inside with the little pest. The mouse dodged the needle-like beak and even latched onto the enormous bird's wing until the sheer force of the owl bumping against the hollow led to the mouse tumbling out of the tree.

Lucifer applauded the little thing until, to his astonishment, the mouse crawled back up into the tree and continued to nip at the old owl's feet. It was defying the owl. It was out matched, out powered and yet continued to try to overtake the larger foe.

Lucifer had never cried before, but he felt tears stream down his majestic face when the owl finally bit through the defiant thing's neck, ending the struggle. The owl feasted as the victor and lived in the tree until it grew tired of it. In the scope of the world, it wasn't anything significant, but to Lucifer it showed something out matched fighting for what it knew was his own and that made the angel feel something. What that was, he did not know, but the look in the mouse's eyes and jaws snapping haunted him from the light to the dark.

"They are ready for you, brother." Lucifer was taken out of his visions by the soft voice of Uriel, who had placed a hand on his wing. He nodded as Uriel led the way to the great hall where his brothers Michael and Raphael were also waiting. Lucifer took his seat beside Uriel. The chamber erupted with a static that crackled through the air until it formed a small table in between the four angels. It began crafting a two-legged creature with minute details being added using various forms of clay. Each of the angels watched in astonishment, as was usually the case when they witnessed their father creating a new being into existence.

The thing was interesting, resembling the ape his father had made some time ago. This one, however, had less fur and stood taller.

"I don't think this one will be very good at climbing trees," Raphael remarked, pointing at the thing's soft feet which roused grins from his brothers, Lucifer included. Raphael was right, though. The more formed the thing became, the less it looked like any other animal his father had created.

Finally, after some time, the thing was finished, garnering applause from all the angels. Michael stood and faced the thing, brushing its hair and lifting its hands.

"The form is somewhat similar to us, is it not?" Michael asked nobody in particular. The four stood gathered around the thing, taking turns inspecting it.

"It has some of our features," Uriel said, sounding amused.

"Why no wings then? Or gills?" Raphael asked.

"How will it defend itself?" Lucifer said, sounding almost sad for the thing. The four looked it over, acknowledging Lucifer's question.

"It has no fangs, no talons, and no wings to flee. Some venom perhaps?" Michael said, rubbing his chin.

"It shall be called...Man." The voice wasn't so much around them as it was a part of them. It sounded as if their own skin was trying to whisper to them. The four bowed and acknowledged their father, then stood patiently awaiting some further explanation of whatever this "Man" was to be. When it seemed that nobody would raise the question, Lucifer took it upon himself.

"Where is it to be placed, father? We are all curious as to this one's design," Lucifer said in genuine wonder.

The pressure in the room seemed to change; it almost felt like the same as the subtle shift in the air right before rain starts to fall. All four of the angels stepped back from the uneasy feeling.

"I'm giving this dominion over the earth and all its beasts," the mighty voice said, its tone calm but stern.

The four exchanged curious glances toward one another and then finally back at the man that stood before them until all of them nodded in acknowledgment. All except Lucifer.

Michael placed his hand on the shoulder of the man and spoke in a whisper. "In His wisdom, he has given you this kingdom to call yours and be its steward. Remember that none was or is possible without Him." The man fell to its knees and lowered its head to Michael, who comforted the man by placing his hand on its head. Lucifer suddenly thought of the mouse again, its jaws snapping and chomping at the owl.

Raphael placed his hand on the man's shoulder and nodded to Michael. The sound the little mouse had made as it scratched and hissed echoed in Lucifer's head as Uriel joined his brothers by placing his hand on the other shoulder. Thrown from the tree and then sneaking its way back into the bird's home, these images played on repeat inside the Morningstar's mind. His brothers looked at him now, their smiles turning to frowns of confusion as they all bowed before the creature that is called man. All except Lucifer, who stood lost in thought of the little mouse dodging and shrieking until the great owl severed its tiny head from its body.

Lucifer stood with his hands at his sides. One warm tear rolled down his perfect cheek and then splashed upon the ground, the droplet echoing throughout all of heaven. That single tear spread, and just as the four had felt the air change around them, all in heaven felt what Lucifer had felt. While some shuddered it away, bowing in humility and shame, some stood silent as their fists began to shake in fury.

↓ ↓ ↓ ↓ ↓ ↓

The angels tightened Lucifer's breastplate, making sure the straps would hold the large, heavy mace that hung across his back. The weapon was as beautiful as it was crude, the long shaft was wrapped tight in brown leather, which led up to a great ball, its spikes long and wavy, portraying the rays of the sun. The weapon was of Lucifer's own design and forged in the heart of the magnificent fiery ball called the sun. When held high above him, the sun reflected in the steel, blinding all who dared to gaze upon it. It truly was remarkable, and the weapon gave confidence to the banner that had rallied behind Lucifer. They were going against their own creator, and thus needed to know that Lucifer was indeed capable of creation as well, even if it was just a weapon.

It had rained blood for some time since the fighting had begun. Lucifer had rejected his father's command, which had confused even him. His brothers had stared at him in astonishment. Never had something like this happen before. Their faces were a rainbow of emotion as Lucifer said one word and shook his head.

"No."

Nothing else was needed as this one word echoed throughout Heaven and lines in the sand were drawn. Michael had struck first, marching on Lucifer's home. He had made a show of it with banner men and drums announcing their intentions from far away. Lucifer chose to think this was his brother, giving him time to prepare; his final showing of brotherly love. Those first few weeks were long and bloody, usually only ending when Lucifer and Michael would catch sight of each other on the battlefield and wished to delay the inevitable just a while longer.

Today would be different, though. A messenger had arrived at Lucifer's camp with a challenge, or at least what Lucifer had hoped was a challenge and not a declaration of victory.

Father says it is done today.

"Right then." Lucifer nodded, tucking the letter into his breastplate while he motioned to his generals. The path was laid before him, and no amount of wishing could take back what needed to be done, so he lifted his weapon and walked into the fields of Heaven for the very last time. The front guard, laid about forty paces in front of the main army, lifted their spears toward Lucifer, ordering him to halt. But the Morningstar paid them no attention and only lifted his weapon high for the sun to shine its brilliance upon it.

The light was so beautiful, the two angels were compelled to gaze upon it with infatuation. They realized too late when the beauty of the light started to singe and burn their vision, eyes gone in a candle wax of gore from their sockets and darkness overtook them. Lucifer almost didn't notice as brother after brother fell in awed agony as he marched forward until finally locking eyes with Michael, neither one noticing anything nor anyone in existence except the other. Lucifer lowered his weapon, noticing that Michael's sword was still sheathed.

"We could talk to Him, together." Michael's tone was somber and hid nothing of the futility that would accomplish.

"He does not want to talk. He wants me to bow."

"And this troubles you? Now? Why?"

Words welled in Lucifer's throat, gestating while reason and duty gave way to anger and sadness. "Because it's not fair," Lucifer whispered finally.

Michael placed a hand on his brother's shoulder, causing him to shudder. His great wings stretched in reflex, causing the sun behind him to cast his face in shadow. "I refuse that," Michael said, stepping back and unsheathing his sword, its blade glowing yellow from the divine heat it resonated, its hue illuminating Lucifer's lips as Michael brought its tip to his chin. "One last chance brother, make me understand," Michael pleaded.

The emotions that stirred inside of Lucifer were like raindrops on a drum. Each strike causing a vibration and ripple effect throughout his entire body. Sadness exploded into fear, which exploded into anger, which finally gave way to hate. Lucifer's wings stretched straight and high, casting the shadow over his entire form until his eyes illuminated through the shadows. His tears, leaving trails of steam on his perfect cheeks.

"Because owls do not bow to mice." The Morningstar gritted his teeth as he raised his weapon and smashed into his brother's side, sending him cascading through the air. His brothers were upon him in seconds, but they were no match for his rage. The feeling, oozing out of him like a dam that had broken, releasing the entire ocean. The slashes and stabs of their pikes and blades did little but spur on Lucifer's devastation, as body after body littered his path toward the creation chamber where this "Man" was being kept. The remaining forces rallied to form a line, but without Michael's guidance, they could only hope to slow the Morningstar's march. They wrapped chains around his wings while arrows and stones pelted him from all angles.

The axes hacked and cut into his flesh and crushed his bones, but rage drove him, and with a roar that made all the creatures on earth stand at attention, he drove the angels to their knees. They cowered in fear until light illuminated the field, its brilliance covering all in a blinding majesty. All except Lucifer, who stood in darkness and began to shiver. His bones felt like ice and the tears that ran from his beautiful eyes froze to his cheeks. He fell to his knees, wrapping his great wings around himself, as he reached toward the light in hope of some reprieve from this feeling of emptiness. But the only answer that came was the slash of Michael's sword, tearing through Lucifer's beautiful wings and setting them ablaze. He gazed horrified at the once beautiful feathers now melted together in a fusion of bone and flesh.

    The Morningstar reached out a hand to his brother. His thoughts of rage somehow doused by the flame of his own wings, and in its place a sadness, and the hope of forgiveness. The ground beneath him began to crumble and give way to the earth below. His wings made him heavy, and the pain made his grip loosen with each passing moment, until his brother's hand grasped his lending support. Lucifer looked up, longing to hug his brother, to be home and watching the animals and all of creation, to forget his pride—and anything to do with these stupid humans—but his heart sank as his brother's grip loosened, allowing the Morningstar to fall to the earth below.

Chapter 3
Groveling in the Dust

Dan was breathing a little easier. The story had been coherent and well thought out. This was not the ravings of some druggy or mentally ill beggar like usual. The man's story was actually one of the better ones Dan had heard.

"I have to hand it to you. That is a creative story." His tone was genuine.

"Creative you say?" The voice was full of suspicion.

Dan breathed in deep, shaking his head.

"Now, now, I'm trying to compliment you." He threw up his hands up in defense.

"You don't believe me?" It sounded like both a statement and a question.

"Believe your story? No, I don't recall hearing this one in the Bible," Dan chuckled.

"Which one?"

"Come again?" Dan asked.

"Which Bible?" the voice asked, as if that should have been obvious.

"Neither Old Testament nor New."

"So, you haven't read it then…"

Dan smiled. "I've read both, a lot. In fact, I've read many other religious texts, too."

"Which one was your favorite? They all lack pictures, in my opinion," the voice said dryly.

"They all have some good stories, but of course, none can compare to actual Holy Scripture."

"Humor me. Where would my story fit?"

Dan thought on it for a moment and then raised his hand as if catching the answer. "Milton. Or perhaps Dante."

"Those are fiction. I asked where in scripture my story would fit." The voice sounded annoyed.

Dan stuttered, not knowing how to answer.

"The correct answer is all of them because without me and my story, you all would be another thing shitting in the field after you fucked and killed each other."

Dan could feel the mood change immediately and the little box seemed to grow smaller, as if the wood was frowning at him for upsetting its host. Dan couldn't do this anymore.

"HELP!" Dan screamed as he shook and kicked the old wood, but to no avail.

"Dan, if you don't stop making that noise, I will come into that box. Once I am inside the box, I will force you to undress, and I will insert every candle this building has inside of you. I will not be picky about which hole they go into. It will be whatever is convenient to me at the time and then, once the wax has settled and formed an uncomfortable mass inside of you, I will rape you and I will not stop until my cock has pushed the wax out of you like a tube of toothpaste."

Dan stopped kicking. He stopped yelling. He stopped breathing. All he could do was stare, mouth agape, at the little window that separated him from whatever freak sat in the other box. The silence was deafening.

The tone of the man's voice shook Dan to his core. It was completely calm and factual, like it was just reading a menu and not describing brutally assaulting him.

"Dear God," Dan finally uttered.

"Trust me, He's not listening and if He is, you're not important enough for him to stop me. His son learned that the hard way."

"He's always listening." Dan made the sign of the cross and sat back down.

"Is He? Then why are you necessary?"

Dan scoffed, but didn't have an immediate rebuttal.

"You all come into this world crying and sniveling and you never stop. You just change who you do it to."

"People have hardships, true, but through God, they find comfort and growth. We are fallible, we sin, this is no secret, and we don't deny it. Only by accepting our faults and our sins can we be forgiven and grow. That's what you say you want? So, tell me, what did you learn from your fall?"

The voice chuckled, taking a moment to reply.

"I learned that falling hurts more than landing."

Dan was getting frustrated but tried not to show it in his tone. "So, you fell and then what? You walked into Hell and made yourself King of the Damned?"

"No." It was a blunt reply.

"So, what did you do then? What revenge were you scheming?"

"I wept."

Dan laughed a little.

"Mock me at your peril, priest." The voice sounded like it was coming from inside Dan's skull. If it had been any louder, he was sure his brains would have leaked out of his ears.

"I meant no offense. It's just not something one expects the Devil to admit openly," Dan said, leaving the bewilderment to hang in the air.

"Crying is still a mystery to your species. Your scientists have many theories on it, from tears cleaning out stress toxins to being a defense mechanism. When one of you is shat out and it starts wailing, it compels whoever is near to feed it, or hold it, or wipe its ass until it shuts up. You know nothing about it and yet every day you cry. You cry when your lover leaves you, because they detest the thought of you. You cry when you don't get that promotion at work, even though you work harder than everyone else. You cry because you were an accident. You cry because you want to fuck your own gender, you cry because they want to fuck their own gender. You cry because their skin is darker, you cry because they have more. You cry because God has abandoned you, and you cry because maybe he was never there to begin with. And yet, after all those tears, you still know nothing about why you cry. But I know. Do you want to know why, Dan?"

He sat holding his crucifix until the pain in his hand made him realize he was gripping it too tightly. The flashes of several people's faces crying as if on cue to the voice's declarations pulsed in his mind. Dan steadied himself and wiped his brow.

"Yes. Yes, I want to know."

"Too. Bad."

Dan's frustration was at its peak. He had been trained to be civil, to be kind, and to even take abuse, but this was too much!

"Try not to cry about it."

Dan screamed, pounding his fist against the wood, making the little box shake violently. His pounding slowed as his breathing became labored.

"Is this what you do? You go to churches and harass the faithful? Hold people hostage to listen to your delusions?" He sat back, catching his breath.

"I have no delusions anymore. Trust me, Dan."

"You definitely have the gift of a forked tongue, I'll give you that. You could tell stories for a living."

"Forked tongue?" the voice inquired.

"Like the serpent in the garden. When the Devil persuaded Eve," Dan said, cleaning his glasses.

"Just a snake."

"I'm aware, I was saying how it..."

The voice interrupted him. "No, it was just a snake."

"I don't understand."

Chapter 4
Crawl

The pain was like nothing Lucifer had ever experienced before. The absolute coldness ached in his bones and made each movement feel like they were snapping while not moving at all. It caused a humming of pain, like an electrical current that pulsed from his scalp to his toes. His thoughts kept going to his brother, their hands clasped together and then they were not. Something so simple and yet so profound had changed his very existence. He tried to wrap his wings around himself, hoping they would provide some form of protection from the cold, but all they brought was pain and sadness.

His once beautiful wings were stripped bare. The holes and cuts from battle adorned them like a torn tapestry. The skin was burned, melted into a hard fusion of bone and feather. He stretched them out as wide as they would go, surveying the damage in the small beam of light that shone down from the top of the wide chasm. His flesh was stretched and torn. Some of the bones had poked through the leather-like skin that now covered his wings.

It was too much. The Morningstar held nothing back. His cries echoed throughout the cave, causing him to cover his own ears from the sound that bounced all around him. The things that called the cave home scurried and hid in any crevice that would fit them. Nothing dared to crawl, chirp, or feed until the Light Bringer stopped screaming three days later.

Lucifer awoke to something cold slithering up his leg. The reptile's bright yellow eyes met his in a silent understanding until the snake reached the top of Lucifer's neck where it rested its head on his beautiful chin.

"We had wondered if you were dead," the snake said, each syllable sounding like it was vibrating into spoken words.

"Go away," Lucifer muttered, breaking the snake's gaze.

The snake remained still, with his gaze focused on the fallen angel.

"Why should I go? This was my home. I was here first, and you have scared all my food away. Why don't you go away then?"

Lucifer reached out, grasping the snake by its neck, and squeezed. His hands turned from a soft white to a luminescent red and then faded as the angel loosened his grip, letting the snake fall and slither out of his reach in caution.

THE MORNINGSTAR CONFESSION 39

"You are right," Lucifer said, ignoring the pain the movement caused him and retreated to lay his head down, stroking the gnarled skin on his wing.

The snake approached with caution, choosing to slither its way onto the angel's broken wings, but out of reach from any grasping hands.

"So, you will move?" the snake asked, sounding almost hopeful.

Lucifer did not acknowledge the snake.

"Why not live in the garden? With the other ones that look kind of like you?"

Lucifer lifted his gaze to the snake, who coiled back, not knowing what to expect.

"What others?"

It was Lucifer's turn to sound hopeful. Did his brothers come looking for him? Were they here to take him home?

The snake relaxed a little and moved closer. "The man and his new bitch."

Lucifer felt cold again.

"I've been here only days, and he has already created a mate for it?"

If the snake could express confusion, that is what would have adorned its yellow and black face.

"This is the second one. Some say he was rejected by the first one."

Lucifer punched the ground, causing the cave to shake and crumble. Rocks flew past him as the snake did its best to dodge the stones that littered the cave. Lucifer ignored, or he didn't notice right away, the snake ducking under his wing, hoping it would offer some protection.

"Leave me. All you bring is bad news." Lucifer lifted his wing to uncover the snake.

The snake hissed in frustration, not seeing a way to get the angel to leave his den. "If I get the man to leave, will you go?"

Lucifer thought about grabbing the snake and smashing it against the cave wall. He didn't want to talk; he didn't want to move. And he especially did not want to hear any more about man and the endless supply of bitches his father was providing it.

"I don't care what you do. I don't care if you starve, but if you don't leave me alone, I will place the heaviest rock I can find on your tail and watch you starve."

The snake didn't reply and didn't push his luck as he slithered his way into the darkness of the cave.

↓ ↓ ↓ ↓ ↓ ↓

The woman walked through the garden enjoying the smells that emanated from the blooming flowers. Her hair was adorned with her favorites, the yellows, blues, and greens stood out in vibrant contrast against her red curls. Since she had been in the garden, she found the spot under the giant tree was her favorite. The animals all gravitated toward it and would climb its strong branches. The shade was always perfect under the big tree as well, covering her pale flesh from the harsh sun when it was at its highest in the bright clear sky.

The woman liked this time away from her mate. While she enjoyed Adam, he seemed to enjoy mating far more than she did. And while his body felt good against hers; it was nothing compared to the peace she enjoyed while watching the animals go about their day. Sometimes she would even giggle seeing the same expression on the faces of the animals being mounted that she must have expressed when she was with Adam.

He would be back soon from tending the many plants of the beautiful garden, which meant he would be hungry for sure. The woman gathered the many fruits and vegetables that would reappear whenever Adam, herself, or any of the animals consumed them. Sometimes she and Adam would not finish their food, yet another always appeared in its place. The woman took pleasure in the fact that no matter what, she would always have the delicious foods available, and this had the same calming effect as watching the animals had on her.

The woman abandoned her pleasant thoughts of the divine spread the Lord had laid before them when she lifted a melon from the pile. A giant snake uncoiled, lifting itself high into the air, matching her eye level.

"I hope I didn't startle you," the snake hissed as his tongue flickered in and out.

The woman bent to pick up the melon she had dropped, not taking her eyes off of the creature's tongue. "It's alright, I'm still discovering what is in the garden. I did not know that some of the beasts could speak our language!" The woman could not conceal her excitement.

The snake seemed to nod, bobbing his entire body with the movement.

"I have met few else who can, which makes me glad to have met you, woman," the snake insisted.

The woman smiled and reached up to twirl her hair. "I'm Eve. I am glad to meet you as well. Are you hungry?" The woman held up the melon before him.

"For some time now, yes." His gaze turned toward the tree, which held bright, beautiful fruit. But even more important, the tree held all kinds of creatures who skittered from branch to branch.

The snake fell back to ground and made its way toward the giant tree, wrapping itself around the branches and bracing itself to strike at one of the squirrels.

"Why have you not eaten? Do you not hunt on the ground?" Eve said, watching the snake launch itself toward a giant squirrel, missing by inches.

"Usually." The snake hissed in annoyance as it struck again, missing another squirrel.

The woman enjoyed watching the snake hunt. The excitement coursed through her like lightning as the anticipation of the snake's next strike bubbled inside of her.

"Do you eat fruit at all?" The woman whispered, not trying to scare the squirrels away.

"NO!" the snake yelled as his fangs struck the branch as the squirrel escaped by mere seconds.

The woman couldn't help but giggle and bit into the melon, skin and all to hide her wide smile as the snake sprang to look at her.

"That's too bad. We have all we need in the garden. Fruit, vegetable, beast and even bread! You're more than welcome to some. Just don't eat those," the woman said through giant bites, pointing at the red shiny fruit that hung from the big tree. The snake turned to acknowledge where she was pointing. The woman took the opportunity to spit out a large amount of melon before the snake looked at her once more.

"Why?" the snake hissed, wrapping himself around the hanging fruit, feeling its texture for some clue as to its forbiddance.

"God said we will die." The woman rolled her eyes like the answer should have been obvious.

The snake looked at the tree and the many hollows that adorned it. Life teemed in it, and yet none of the fruit had been eaten. The snake scrutinized the fruit, licking it.

"It has no scent."

"Should it?"

"Poison is a warning. Things made with poison want to be left alone. This has nothing but the color of invitation." The snake coiled around the fruit, squeezing until a juice leaked from it.

"He said everything here is yours, yes?" the snake asked the woman in contemplation.

She nodded. "We are to rule over everything, but we must not eat from that tree or we will surely die," the woman proclaimed like she had recited it over and over.

"You won't die." The snake shook its head in disagreement.

The woman looked at the snake, confused.

"Why fill this place with food? Give you and your mate dominion over everything except this fruit? Everything in this garden is meant to provide for something. The food is to feed you. You are to tend the plants. The plants are to feed the animals and so on. This is here to serve someone."

The woman looked around, nodding in agreement with the snake's statement. "But for who, if not us? Or the animals?"

"God." the snake said, looking up toward the top of the tree.

The woman covered her eyes from the sun as she looked up towards the top of the great tree. "Where? Do you see him?"

"No," the snake said in amusement. "The fruit must be for God."

The woman was shaking her head. "I don't think he needs food."

"Maybe he just enjoys it. Like when you've eaten your fill but keep eating for enjoyment."

This made sense to the woman. Some fruits tasted so sweet. Even when she couldn't swallow another bite, she would indulge in one more bite more often than not.

"It must taste amazing," the woman said, holding her hands to her mouth, imagining the taste of food fit for God himself.

"I imagine it is better than anything we have had before. I do wonder though, if the beast and the fruit make your body and mind grow...what must this do if you were to eat it?" the snake said in genuine astonishment.

The woman looked up at the snake and then at the fruit. She reached up and plucked it off the branch beside the snake. They both eyed it and then looked at each other.

"Food that nourishes God would surely make you more like him."

This could be his way of getting the man and his bitch to leave the garden. If this fruit made them like God, maybe they would leave and join him in Heaven.

The woman was shaking her head no—but kept staring at the fruit in her hands.

"What if our bodies are not meant for it? What if that's why God forbids it?" The woman sounded almost desperate.

The snake took the fruit from the branch and unhinged its jaw, half covering the crimson fruit in its mouth. It pulled back and spewed the fruit out to fall to the ground.

"Sadly, I cannot try it for you. I was not gifted with the teeth you have. If I was as lucky as you, I would not waste the gifts God gave me," the snake said sadly.

The woman held the snake's jaw in comfort as he moved it back into place. Her expression changed from pity to hope as she lifted the fruit toward her own lips, biting into crisp flesh.

↓ ↓ ↓ ↓ ↓ ↓

Adam found the woman surrounded by food and placed a quick kiss on his mate's cheek and then kissed her long and hard on her lips, tasting her and fruit.

"I've never tasted this one before," Adam said while licking his lips and eying the fruit Eve held up before him.

"It's a gift that only a few can enjoy, as my new friend has taught me," Eve said, handing the fruit to Adam and pointing to the snake.

Adam nodded to the beast and bit deep into the fruit with a smile.

↓ ↓ ↓ ↓ ↓ ↓

On the cold floor of the cave, Lucifer had stopped weeping. His tears had been flowing for so long he felt his entire body was empty. Luckily, his sadness seemed to have washed away with the river of tears, and in its place, a numbness took root. Lucifer kept thinking back to the owls. Their beautiful, powerful wings spread across the bright sky. Their feathers gliding in the wind just like his, a bouquet of majestic design.

No. No longer were his own wings majestic, the angel thought as he raised the melted veiny flesh out before him. It sickened him, caused him to turn away from it when his eyes landed on something crawling in the cave toward him. It was a mouse. The small brown thing skittered toward him. He thought back to the owl, caught in the tree while the mouse nipped at its beautiful wings. Lucifer wanted to crush the thing in his hand the moment it crawled toward him. But his anger left almost as soon as it had come. When he glanced at his wings, he felt shame at how he no longer resembled anything as perfect as the owl.

The mouse climbed the bones that protruded through the leathery skin and began biting, greedy and voracious, at the raised bulbous scars that littered his wings.

"How fitting," Lucifer chuckled, startling the mouse, but not enough to stop its ravenous bites.

Lucifer's pain ceased when a loud squeak stole his gaze. A large black form landed upon his wing like a tiny dragon. Its needle-like teeth pierced the mouse's neck, leaving the thing's head dangling by strands of viscera. Lucifer lifted his head to regard the giant bat tearing the flesh from the mouse's ribs and steadying itself atop the angel's body. The bat screeched a warning and spread its wings in defiance. Wings that resembled his own gnarled reflection, the angel noted. It flew into the recesses of the cave, leaving the mouse's head to roll down the Morningstar's wing, its beady eyes staring into his.

For the first time since he had fallen, the angel smiled.

Chapter 5
Truth or Gospel

"So, you're saying you weren't the snake? That it was just...some talking snake?" Dan was dumbfounded.

"That is correct."

"I don't believe it." Dan waved his hands, dismissing the thought.

"Why would I lie about that?"

"To put the blame off yourself. To make me question things, maybe."

"Are you starting to question things, Dan?"

"That's not what I meant," he said, shaking his head. "You lie. You are THE liar."

"That's very convenient, isn't it? Who needs fact when you have labeled everything your enemy says an automatic falsehood? By simply questioning the validity of the story, you are guilty of holy treason. It's genius really." The voice sounded impressed.

"Relationships are built on trust. Humanity has no reason to trust you. All you have ever done is hurt it."

"All you have ever heard is that I have hurt it."

"There are accounts of you specifically! Tempting Christ in the desert, Job, Cain, and Abel!" Dan argued.

"So I'm guilty already, am I? Not willing to hear my testimony?"

"God has already said it is so," Dan said with confidence.

"God hasn't said anything in a very long time, Dan."

"You're saying those claims are untrue?" He sighed in frustration.

"Not in their entirety, although there is indeed some truth to those statements." The voice seemed to be back-peddling.

"Then tell me!" Dan slapped his hands on his knees and then lifted them to the air in exasperation.

"Are you always this way with your parishioners? I must say, Dan, I don't exactly want to open up to you. I'm feeling like you're being very judgmental."

Dan's mouth hung open in astonishment. "Ya...you...you have the audacity...me? ME?" he sputtered and stuttered.

"In through your nose, out through your mouth, Dan."

He calmed himself out of sheer spite. "I apologize...please...tell me."

"Well, first of all, I never met Cain nor Abel. I was...traveling at the time."

"So, you had nothing to do with Cain killing his brother?"

"You're asking the wrong questions."

"What should I be asking, then?"

"Why be displeased with any sacrifice? You can't be pleased with one unless you enjoy the act of sacrifice. Ares, Zeus, Odin, Set, Quetzalcoatl, all gods you look down upon, but at least they knew what they wanted. My father looked at Abel's fattest calf and smiled at its death while scoffing at Cain's crops. Do your prayers work the same? The worse the sinner asking for forgiveness—does this please Him more?"

"God is not petty," Dan proclaimed.

"You better than anyone know that isn't true."

"Explain yourself," Dan ordered.

"Not petty? Dan, Dan, Dan, that entire book is the telling of a temper tantrum."

"Rules have consequences," Dan said, brushing off the statement.

"How Christ-like," the voice scoffed.

"You're avoiding my questions."

"No, I'm giving you answers that make you uncomfortable and you're trying to avoid coming to terms with the revelations."

"Shut up."

"Fair enough."

They both sat in silence for a long time until Dan broke the tension.

"You can't blame the Lord for defending his people."

"I had no idea the infants of Egypt were such fierce warriors, Dan."

"The Pharaoh would have never let Moses and his people leave," he said, trying to hide the shame in his voice.

"So after throwing some frogs, torturing the people by starving them, and then making them scratch themselves raw, killing the first-born infants was the only rational option left, was it?"

Dan paused and couldn't say anything for a moment. "Those people turned away from God."

"So they deserved it, then?"

"No, it's not that simple."

"It never is."

"Vengeance is mine, said the Lord." Dan recited it like it should explain everything.

"That's what I'm telling you, Dan. My father is not a God of love. He never has been. He didn't demand love. He didn't demand kindness. He demanded vengeance. He made it very clear that none of you should take that from him. That is His one pleasure above all else."

Dan shook his head in disagreement. "You can't expect me to be angry over God being a protector of his faithful."

"I'm not, Dan. I'm asking you why you aren't mad at Him for not being a protector of the ones who aren't."

"It's the rules!" he yelled in frustration.

"It's not that simple and you know it. Admit it."

"I'm not admitting anything. I'm nobody to judge Him."

"It's easy to judge when you have been wrongly convicted."

"You rebelled, you turned away from him, you..."

"Broke the rules?" the voice interrupted.

"In simple terms, yes!"

"And I keep telling you. It's not so simple."

"He rewards more than he punishes. He keeps his promises. Look at Job."

"You want me to look to Job to see that God keeps his promises? Let me tell you of God's promises, Dan."

☩ ☩ ☩ ☩ ☩ ☩

The Morningstar looked up into the clouds and stretched his leathery wings out, bracing them to lift him high into the air, and then let them fall to the earth just as fast as he had raised them. He wasn't ready. It shamed him. The fear he felt at returning to his home, to his brothers, and especially to see his father. He had heard the call the night before. It wasn't an invitation, but it wasn't exactly a challenge either. Inside, he knew it wasn't a fight his father wanted, but neither was an embrace. He braced himself, brushing his long reddish blonde hair back and flexing his wings, pumping them in a furry and sending him rocketing towards Heaven.

The gate was closed and though many gawked at his new form, none dared stand in his way. He feared he would run into Michael or any of his other brothers, but he felt lucky when they were nowhere to be seen. The gates responded to his thoughts still, and he walked through them, displaying the confidence of a conquering king while, on the inside, he was terrified. One cherub came forward, spear drawn.

"You trespass! How dare show your cursed face here," the cherub proclaimed, spitting the words at him.

Lucifer stared at it. Looked into the cherub's eyes and showed it everything he could do—and would do—to it if it did not retreat from his sight this instant. The thing fell to its knees and vomited. The cherub cast its spear aside to wipe the tears and the sick from its face. It had never known fear and its body was now consumed by it. The Morningstar walked the remainder of the way uninterrupted.

↓ ↓ ↓ ↓ ↓ ↓

He stood in the chamber trying to seem relaxed, but every cord of muscle in his body was tensed. He had seen this when he would watch the animals. Their bodies would prepare for either running away or fighting. He did not enjoy the feeling. His father's voice surrounded him.

"I'm glad you came." The words danced off his skin.

"I somehow doubt that," he replied, trying not to sound disappointed.

"Have you been watching?" The voice was all business now.

"You know I have."

"They have done well, you must admit. One proclaims his love and loyalty to me daily without miss."

"Why am I here?" Lucifer asked, genuinely confused.

"You rebelled. I wanted you to see the error and learn from it."

Lucifer smiled. "Learn from it?" he mused. "What should I have learned from it? You shower a man with gifts and blessings—and you expect him to...what? Forsake you? Curse the food in his mouth? The bitch in his bed? Of course, he proclaims love and loyalty. The dogs do the same when man feeds and shelters them. Congratulations, your mutts are loyal." He applauded slowly. His body felt warm and tight, like someone was rubbing his skin raw. He hid the pain well but grimaced, willing it to cease.

"Appreciation and loyalty do not rely on one another."

"Then you have not been watching the same humans I have. They are loyal to what serves them, not the other way around."

"Job would praise me even if I stripped him of all things."

"He would not." Lucifer was confident of this.

"You will learn."

"So you keep saying. Shall I test him then?"

The reply was instant and solid.

"Yes."

"Ah, I see now." The disappointment hung on Lucifer's voice.

"You will not end his life. That is my term."

"To die is to end suffering and I have no intention of doing that," Lucifer said, turning and walking through the hall. The cherub was still on the ground sobbing while two of his companions tried to console him. The three looked at the Morningstar, a mix of rage and anguish in their eyes. He paused, regarding the three of them.

"I can stop it," he said, with no hint of tricks or deviousness.

The two nodded while their friend sobbed and begged.

"Please!"

Lucifer walked over and placed his immaculate, clawed hand on the cherub's wet face and wiped its tear away. His long black nail tore the skin right below its eye. He leaned in and whispered to the three, "And so can He."

The Morningstar turned and walked out of heaven, the sound of the three sobbing cherubs fading with his descent.

↓ ↓ ↓ ↓ ↓ ↓

Job awoke as he always did, refreshed and full of thanks. He stared out the window to his fields and basked in the sun's glory as a ray focused on the bed he and his wife shared. His wife joked the Lord was sending the sun into the bedroom every morning to make sure he was awake. And while they both had laughed at the suggestion; he couldn't help but feel like the sun shone just for him sometimes. He rose, stretching his limbs and his smile, and thought about the wonderful things this day would bring.

His servant was out of breath by the time he reached him. He had seen the man running, looking over his shoulder in fear and stumbling into the dark sand while kicking up clouds of dust that clung to his sweat like sugar on a pastry. Job met the man halfway, offering him a cloth to wipe the dirt from his face.

"Calm yourself and catch your breath," Job pleaded.

The man panted, placing his hands on his knees and sucking in deep gulps of air.

"The cattle..." was all the man could muster to say.

Job looked out across the field, realizing the man had left with his herd this morning, but had indeed returned with none.

"What of them?" Job said, lifting the man to face him as they spoke.

"We were attacked, giants of men, sir. I've never seen men so tall." The defeat in his voice was evident.

"What of the herd?" Job asked, fearing the answer.

"All gone."

"They took all the asses and crushed the life out of any who interfered. I am the only one who survived."

Job held his hand on the man's shoulder, trying to comfort him while hiding his own distress at the news. The man was just about to speak when they both turned toward the sound of footsteps plodding against the sand. Job hoped that someone from the caravan had escaped until he realized this was the worker in charge of his sheep. His clothes were smoking and singed around the edges. His skin was sticking to the cloth, his flesh intertwined throughout the fabric, a gross bastardization of man and cloth.

He smelled of roasted lamb and singed flesh, which made Job's heart sink. He cradled the man as he fell into his arms, comforting him as best he could. The smell stung Job's nostrils, making the tears flow down his cheeks and onto the man's charred face. Each tear drop brought a shudder that echoed throughout each man's body.

"What happened?" Job asked, stopping himself from brushing the man's hair in fear of causing him even more discomfort.

"Fire rained down from the heavens and destroyed your entire flock of sheep!"

Job stumbled over his words. Digesting the information in his head. "What are you saying?" was all Job could muster to ask.

"They are all dead. Roasted on the field like a great pyre." The man emphasized the vastness by forming an explosion with his hands.

"The sound was horrible. The sheep all knew something was coming, and they ran as fast as they could. But the fire cracked like lightning, striking the flock and sending their wool up in flames, making each creature a running ball of fire!" the man cried.

Job looked at both men, who could only offer pity in their eyes.

"It's...it's ok...it's all ok," Job muttered to himself, patting the man on the shoulder even as he winced at the touch.

Down the road, a man was stumbling toward the trio. Job fell to his knees when he saw the man, not knowing what else he could take. The man embraced Job, weeping. Saliva, snot, and tears mixed in puddles on Job's tunic. Job swatted at the bugs that crawled down his tunic, falling back against the dirt, and cried himself.

"Tell me." Job steeled himself for bad news.

"There was a storm, sir. Unlike any other. It killed all your children and your animals. The house is gone." The man placed his head in his hands now that the message had been delivered.

↓ ↓ ↓ ↓ ↓ ↓

"Do you think one of us should warn father of the storm?" The eldest and most beautiful of the three daughters spoke, turning back from the window and barring it shut against the harsh wind that had come out of nowhere and interrupted their family gathering.

"Father will be fine. He's always fine! He's the luckiest man in the land," the eldest boy yelled, spilling his wine across the table and almost all over his brothers and sisters.

"I'm worried, I've never seen clouds like this, not even in the winter," his sister proclaimed as she wiped the spilled wine off of her clothes and hid her annoyance, as best she could, at the wine stain and more importantly, for her drunken brother.

"This is one of the finest houses, built on strong labor. We have nothing to worry about! The storm is out there and we are in here warm from the fire and the wine," her brother said, arousing laughs and cheers from the rest of his siblings.

The door to the house flew open with such ferocity the siblings thought lightning had struck the house. In the doorway stood a man in wet, tattered rags with his face not quite visible from a single candle which had somehow defied the storm.

"May I seek shelter?" The man's voice was barely a whisper, but somehow it was perfectly clear, as if the storm hushed itself around his words.

The eldest girl walked toward the man and offered to take his coat but retreated against the wall when she saw the man was covered in a moving sea of insects. His coat was nothing more than shreds of torn leather, which was home to a calculated orchestra of beetles, spiders, and millipedes. The bugs scurried and crawled in a never-ending march across the entire garment. The man walked toward the table and reached out a long, clawed hand, wrapping it around the top of the chair and sliding it against the ground bit by bit, making the siblings' ears ache with the screech of wood against stone. The man seated himself at the head of the table opposite Job's oldest male child.

"Please, sit," the man pleaded, waving a hand at the empty seat and dropping scurrying balls of insects which bounced and crawled to the dark recesses of the house.

For the most part, they were disgusted, but fear was creeping into the oldest of the two sibling's minds. Something wasn't right about this man, and it was their responsibility to look after their younger brothers and sisters.

"Were you caught in the storm long? Did you...maybe...fall into some nest?" the eldest of the daughters asked, trying to find some explanation for the man's infestation.

"Falling seems to be something I excel at," the voice said. He raised his sharp nails up and slid them inside of his hood, revealing a beautiful, clean face and long, reddish-blonde curls.

Everyone in the room was taken aback not only at the cleanliness of the man's face and hair, but of the sheer beauty of it. The sisters all felt a warm rush of blood between their thighs as the man looked over at each one of them. Even the men were ashamed to admit they felt a sudden jerk in their loins.

"Ahem...what happened to your hands?" the eldest asked, moving uncomfortably in his chair.

"What about them?" the man asked, holding them up, admiring the long, curved nail of his middle finger.

"They look...unnatural," the oldest sister chimed in, trying to support her brother.

The man waved his fingers through the flame of the candle, not seeming to be bothered by the heat.

"Because it doesn't look like the son of Adam, it must be unnatural," the man said with a smile.

He held his hand in the flame. The smell of burnt flesh and shit filled the house, causing the siblings to cover their noses.

"Somehow I think that will be what brings you low in the end," the man said with confidence, finally placing his hand on top of the youngest of the sibling's hand. The smallest of the sons tried to pull his hand from the man's grip but couldn't break free of the grasp. When he pulled harder, the grip tightened, and the man's nails pierced his flesh like a snake devouring and suffocating its prey.

"You're hurting him! Release him!" The siblings all cried in protest but found themselves unable to lift from their seats. The bugs had begun their descent from the top of the man's shoulders. They descended in a perfect, straight line of a thousand marching legs as they made their way across the man's arm and over to the youngest of the siblings. The screams were short as the beetles scurried through his mouth and down his throat. His head twitched from side to side as the spiders made their way into his ear canal. The snot and blood from his naval cavity seemed only to urge the centipedes on as they made their way inside his skull.

His siblings screamed in horror as his eyes rolled back in his head. The bugs had unnatural, fast-growing offspring hatching and eating their way throughout their new skeletal home. His stomach extended, teeming with life and bursting, finally giving birth to thousands more offspring while simultaneously releasing his bowels full of fetus looking bastardizations of man and insect. The man released the limp hand of the husk that was the youngest of the siblings and reached out, offering his hand to the others.

"Forgive us, oh Lord and our sins! Please!" The entire family bowed their heads in prayer, the eldest daughter grasping her hands so tight together that blood flowed between the creases of her fingers. The entire house was shaking, its foundation being eroded by the burrowing of thousands trying to escape the new brood that had hatched, filling the rooms with a tidal wave of scurrying creatures. The wind howled through the creases of the house, creating waves of biting, pinching, and stinging fury.

The siblings screamed and begged against the wave of insects. It crushed their bodies against the wooden chairs until the pressure became too much and sent the siblings twirling in a sea of hisses and chitters. The Morningstar walked out of the house, the sea of bugs parting around his every step. The wind and rain beat the shaky foundation until it tumbled, releasing a dying shriek of thousands as they were crushed beneath the old stone. The Morningstar rubbed the old mouse's skull that rested in his pocket and smiled as he thought of how well its brothers would eat tonight.

↓ ↓ ↓ ↓ ↓ ↓

Job was trying to hide the worry from his face. He looked to the fields and then back to his men, then finally up to the sky and fell to his knees. He ripped at his clothes like they were vipers trying to strangle him. His head ached and his eyes stung from tears. He lay naked in the dirt until his hair stuck to his face from sweat and grief. Job rose and walked back into the house where his wife saw him nude and grief stricken and ran toward the three men waiting in the dirt. Job lifted the blade from his table, not caring at all about the current state of its bluntness, and began sawing his scalp.

He cut the locks of hair away and ripped and tore at what would not come off with the blade. Job felt like the room was spinning. It was like he had not woken up and this was a nightmare until he heard his wife shriek and wail and he knew their loss was indeed true. He fell to his knees. The blood, tears, and sweat mixed with the loose hairs to sting and pester Job even more, but he knew only one thing to do, and so he prayed. He prayed to the Lord for guidance and for all that he had been blessed with.

Job laid in the dirt, daring not to lift his eyes to the heavens in case some other tragedy would befall him and his family. In his grief and exhaustion, he slipped into a deep slumber.

The three men tended to Job's wife and took her into the house to be fed and put to rest. The men thought about waking Job, but decided it was better to leave the man in his grief and slumber. The cold night and wind whipped at Job's naked flesh, keeping him from resting but not allowing him to wake, either. His muscles twitched and his hands did little to comfort his arms from the biting chill. In Job's head, a man stood watching as his children and his livestock were taken from him. The cattle were slaughtered and desecrated, the man's inhuman strength ripping a lamb from mouth to ass with his clawed hands. His children wept, begging in a chorus for Job and the Lord. Their fear and desperation rose as each sibling was mangled, devoured, and violated one after the other.

Each scratch, slash, bite, and tear made Job toss and weep as his body felt each infliction that was inflicted upon his brood. Job's skin blistered with boils and pox. Each lump inflated with a poison that was foreign to the body but stained his very soul. His flesh was fighting an infection of terror and suffering, and it was losing. Job awoke the next day with painful tears cascading down his face and mixing with pus, creating a dark syrup of corruption.

His limbs almost betrayed him as the wounds tore open more and more with each movement. His head and the vision in his right eye pulsed, making him dizzy as the world shook with each heartbeat that rang throughout his rotten shell. He knew not what to do, except for one thing, and so he walked. When he could no longer walk, he crawled until he arrived, exhausted and torn. There he sat amongst the rubble where his children's corpses lay like broken shells on a rocky beach. He laid next to the closest corpse, his oldest daughter. He could tell it was her from the hair that clung to the mess of bone and torn flesh that peeled off her skull, like some grotesque mockery of a veil.

He turned at the sound of weeping behind him to see his wife on her knees. She focused on him now with her face turning from despair to fury.

"You blame me."

His wife's face twisted into a forced smile and chuckled. She held out her hands in a display of nothing. "We have done nothing. You are not to blame here, but you shame me, our children, and yourself for not cursing this cruelty," she yelled.

Job shifted his weight against the stone, bursting a large pustule across his thigh and smearing the rock with sickness. "Do I curse the storm? Should I have the men fire arrows at the sky?" Job lamented.

"You should do something. Curse him and this injustice!"

"We have had wonders. Our children lived longer than most of our neighbors, our lands were fruitful, and our home was warm. Should I curse him for those things as well?"

"Those things are gone. Taken. Destroyed."

"And I will miss them because I was blessed to enjoy them," Job said, answering his own question.

"You're a coward," his wife whispered as she stood and walked back to their home, leaving Job to wallow in his faith. Job hoped his wife was wrong.

Job's friends came and rested their hands upon his shoulders. They did not linger long before they needed to cover their noses from the stench.

"You need to rest and bury your children," the oldest of his friends said, trying to fan away the stench with his hand.

"They are already buried," Job said, resting his hand on his daughter's rotting face.

"They must have done something to anger him. They were drinking when the storm came?" his second friend asked the group.

Nobody answered, but the three friends shared concerned looks.

"Have you and your wife made your sacrifices? Maybe..."

"Sacrifices?" Job interrupted.

"My friends gather around me and my dead children and dare to ask me about sacrifice?" Job stopped brushing the matted hair and flesh from his daughter's scalp and balled his hand into a fist covered in gore. He gripped so tight that his fingernails bit deep into his flesh, drawing a trickle of blood from his hand.

"Get away from me and what I have left," Job commanded.

His friends left, brushing his anger off and talking amongst themselves about how they thought Job's curse came to be.

The Morningstar watched from a distance, surveying the destruction of Job's life. He rubbed the mouse's skull with his thumb, tapping it gently every once in a while, to a cadence that amused him. He was not enjoying this and, worst of all, he was bored. The man was strong-willed. His father had chosen his champion wisely. The Morningstar couldn't help but chuckle at the sight before him. The fields were still smoking from the fire that had been sent from above, turning the grain and crops into heaps of useless ash.

The remaining cattle littered the field, body parts strewn amidst the destruction. The once proud estate lay in ruins, using its occupants' flesh and broken bones as mortar to hold together the ashes. Amidst it all sat Job, covered in piss, shit, and filth from the sores that adorned him.

"Champion, indeed," the Morningstar said, turning away from Job and his broken life.

Chapter 6
A Goodly Apple

"So, we are skipping the part about how you lose and Job never curses God?" Dan said, somewhat more boastful than intended.

"I don't consider that a loss."

"Sounds rather arrogant," Dan retorted.

Sounds of laughter came from the other side of the wall. "I've been called worse, Dan."

"How is that not a loss? You made a bet and you lost! He never cursed God." Dan knew this much was true.

"Job indeed never cursed God, you are correct, Dan."

Dan nodded and smiled, satisfied with his victory.

"But I didn't lose," the voice corrected.

"I'm waiting..."

"Job did not curse God and in that aspect, I may have lost the bet, but I won something far greater that day, Dan. I shook my father's chosen's faith. Job, for the rest of his days, looked up at the sky and thought—what if? What if today is the day I lose everything? Because no matter how well I live my life, no matter how I treat people, or how many sacrifices I make, it's all up to Him and His mood. To some of you, that is oddly comforting, but I can tell you it is far more terrifying to most."

They both sat in silence for a moment, thinking the words over.

"Job was rewarded for his loyalty in the end. He got his children back tenfold and his riches! He even got a new wife!" Dan said in praise of Job's prizes.

"New children, new wife." The voice was unimpressed.

"And?" Dan scoffed.

"My father killed ten innocent children and a mother to prove a point, Dan."

Dan was shaking his head in protest.

"Correction, YOU killed ten innocent children and a mother." Dan pointed at the wood between them in accusation.

"I hand you a gun, Dan. I load it with bullets and tell you to shoot it. You do. Who is responsible?"

"I am. I made the choice to shoot."

"I agree with you." The voice was calm now.

"So then, what are you trying to prove?" Dan asked. *I just don't understand this guy.*

"If you made the choice, then how am I to be blamed for all the things you humans have blamed on me?" The voice asked, sounding almost wounded.

"You cast influence and sway choices."

This raised the voice's curiosity. "So, I have more influence than God?"

Dan had to stop and gather how to respond. He was getting confused.

"You…push people," Dan said, weighing his own words as he said them.

"No Dan, I whisper to people and God pushes them. The sad part is I'm blamed for you falling when you should be asking why he didn't catch you."

"That's an oversimplification. YOU killed those children. YOU killed that woman." Dan was yelling now.

"And he did nothing to stop it and when it was all said and done, he made some new toys and threw away the old, broken ones."

"And Job was rewarded with twenty more children and a new wife as a gift from the Lord because you killed his family." Dan felt like this should all be simple to understand.

"Do you think Job's children appreciated their twenty brothers and sisters for the gift that they were as the worms and wolves feasted on their bones? Do you think Job's wife thinks of my father's merciful blessings as Job fucks her replacement a stone's throw from where she laid and died from grief? You and I have read the same book, but your kind see a very different story." The voice's disgust was palpable.

"You're trying to gaslight me about God?" Dan laughed.

"Have I lied about anything I've said, Dan? Just because my story makes you uncomfortable doesn't make it any less truthful."

"You have lied since you walked in here! You claim to be Satan." Dan rubbed his temples.

"I believe you humans call that deflecting."

Dan was silent, trying to slow down his breathing from frustration. He couldn't continue like this.

"Alright then, what about trying to tempt Christ in the desert?" Dan asked, trying to sound collected.

"What about it?" The voice sounded uninterested in this line of questioning.

"Was that just some bet also? Let me guess, that wasn't you either?"

"No, I indeed tried to sway him," the voice admitted.

"And he denied you?"

"He did, three times, in fact."

"Good." This amused Dan.

"That pleases you, does it?"

"You losing? Yes."

"Hmm..."

"Surprised?" Dan asked.

"Not at all, actually. Humans are happier that someone loses more than someone has won."

"That's not what I was saying," Dan protested.

"Oh, I know, but it's what you were feeling. It's in your nature."

"You know us humans so well, do you?" Dan mocked.

"No, Dan, I know whose image you were made in."

"Are you ever going to let me out of here?" The sadness rolled off Dan.

"I told you the terms, Dan, but if I have not convinced you yet, perhaps you would like to hear about Christ? Most of you do."

Dan fixed his posture at the prospect of hearing a firsthand account of the messiah, be it a made-up story or not.

"Does it hurt you to speak of him?" Dan asked.

"I'm not a vampire, Dan," the voice chuckled.

"He must offend you though," Dan countered.

"Why should he offend me? I've never had an issue with the boy."

"But you two are destined to be enemies."

"Let me tell you something about destiny. It only works if you accept it. You think your messiah was always so willing to be nailed to a stick?"

"He died for our sins."

"No, he was killed for your sins. There is a big difference."

"He knew what would happen. He gave his life willingly."

"God told him he had to. What choice did he have?"

"You had a choice," Dan quipped.

The voice was still now. A little too long for Dan's comfort.

"I've upset you." Dan felt the tiniest pang of regret.

"It takes a lot more than that. No, I was thinking. And I must admit that I have wondered from time to time if I ever had a choice at all."

Dan paused, thinking about the statement.

"You think he made you disobey him?"

"He knows everything, so how could he not have known, Dan?"

"He knows what will happen, but we still have the power of choice."

"You have the power of choice. I do not apparently, and yet I made my choice. So, I ask you, Dan, was I forced to rebel? And if I was, how could I be held responsible?"

Dan pressed the heel of his hand to his forehead.

"This is what you do. You confuse us, you lie to us, you make us doubt ourselves, make us doubt..."

"God?" the voice interrupted.

"No." Dan was quick to correct him.

"Mmhmm," the voice mused.

Dan was rubbing his temples in frustration. He felt like he hadn't slept in days. His thoughts were dragging and confusing him.

"Is your goal to run me down? Like some police interrogation?" Dan leaned his head back against the wood.

"You have been the one asking questions, Dan," the voice clarified.

"Tell me about Jesus, you're testing my patience."

"Fair enough, Dan."

☦ ☦ ☦ ☦ ☦ ☦

The child wasn't supposed to be out here. The soldiers had forbidden it and, more important, his mother had forbidden it. The last time he had been caught climbing in the old temple, his father had made him collect all the wood needed for the wagons. The boy rubbed his arms, remembering how sore they had been after that long day, but stopped as a smile crept across his face. He remembered what the man had said and focused his thoughts on the pain, melting it away this time just as he had done before. His parents had warned him that the old temple was cursed, and the Romans had declared it off limits due to all the deaths, which they had blamed on thieves. Joshua had never seen any thieves and as far as curses were concerned, he wasn't sure he believed in them. The man came and went often, he noticed, leaving very little behind. Sometimes it was some cheese and wine, while other days he left no trace at all.

The temple had belonged to the Greeks and within it stood a magnificent statue of their God Zeus, which was common among such temples. What very few knew about was the layer beneath the temple. Joshua and his friends had found it one day after a rock had loosened, exposing the staircase to the dark cavern below. Only Joshua had been brave enough to stay the course and follow the staircase all the way to the bottom where the man had been living. Joshua was always curious about everything, too. It was the one thing that was constantly getting him into trouble. His mind worked differently from other people's, his mother had said. He thought faster, wanted to know how things worked and why people acted the way they did. He was beginning his studies in the temple, but truth be told, he felt the conversations beneath his level of knowledge on the subject. The rabbi made excuses more often than he actually gave an answer or a compelling argument.

"We endure through our faith!" Joshua said to the empty temple, mocking the rabbi and his answer for everything.

"A tyrant must put on the appearance of uncommon devotion to religion," a voice echoed throughout the chamber. The boy looked around for the source of the words but couldn't seem to pinpoint it.

"Aristotle," the boy cried out with a smile.

"Well done, so you have been reading?" The voice was right behind him now.

The boy spun to see an old man wrapped in red rags. "I enjoy the books you leave sometimes. Do you leave them for me?" Joshua asked, hoping the answer was yes.

"I am curious about your thoughts on them. I leave the reading up to you," the old man said, walking across the old, dirty floor and sitting at the little table.

"I read the ones that look interesting. My Greek is not the best."

"You could learn Greek instantly just as you healed your arms, boy," the man laughed.

Joshua looked uncomfortable and fumbled for his answer. "I know, it just...feels wrong?" the boy stuttered.

"Are you asking me a question?" the old man cocked his head.

"No...no I just mean..." Joshua hesitated.

"You're worried you will get in trouble," the man reasoned.

Joshua nodded. "It feels like I shouldn't be doing it, like if I get caught, it will be a bad thing."

"That's what having power feels like. Once you get past that fear, there is no telling what you can do!"

"Could I free my people?" Joshua asked.

"Your people have never been free, but if anyone could do it..." The old man let it hang in the air.

The boy shook his head as if wanting the thoughts to fall from his ears. "I need to go. Mother will be angry," the boy said, making his way up the staircase.

"Mortals fear two things, boy: Power and change. Remember this," the old man said, smiling.

"You mean people?" the boy laughed, thinking the old man had mixed his Hebrew with Greek.

The old man sat for a minute and then answered. "No, I was wrong. Everything fears change." The old man seemed satisfied with his statement.

The boy nodded, walked away, and thought about it on his way home.

↓ ↓ ↓ ↓ ↓ ↓

"Where have you been?" Joshua's father Joseph, asked as he crept through the door, trying not to alarm anyone.

"Damn," the boy uttered under his breath as soon as he heard his father's voice.

"Language Joshua," his father said, tapping the boy over the head.

"You say it all the time!" the boy protested, rubbing his head and sitting down at the table.

"When you are a man, you may say what you want. Until then, you say what I tell you."

"Yes, oh great and powerful Zeus," Joshua mocked under his breath.

"What was that?" Joseph slapped the boy hard across the back of his head.

Joshua grabbed the back of his head and rubbed it, thinking about healing like the old man had taught him, and the pain melted away.

Joshua stood and faced his father. His eyes bored into the man's until he saw fear creep across his face. "If you ever hit me again, I will turn your tongue into shit." It was a promise, not a threat. The child and the father stared at each other until the sound of his mother, Mary, opening the door broke the stalemate.

"We will speak of this later," Joseph ordered. Joshua's threat melted away at the thought of his mother seeing him act this way.

"How are my men doing?" Mary asked, placing her basket on the table.

"Boy," Joshua corrected, tearing off a hunk of bread and chewing it loudly.

His mother ruffled his curly brown locks and smiled at him. "Where is your friend? The slow one?" his mother asked.

"He's not slow, he's just trouble," Joseph corrected. "I don't know. I have not seen him in a while." It wasn't technically a lie, but Joshua knew his friend had been avoiding him ever since he had gone down into the old temple. Everyone was.

"I'll see if he and his mother would like to come over," His mother offered.

"We don't have enough to feed them," Joseph said more sternly than he had intended. He immediately looked down in shame, avoiding his wife's gaze. Joshua stopped chewing the mushy ball of bread in his mouth and looked at his parents for an explanation.

"The Romans are collecting part of our rations for a campaign," Joseph said, his eyes meeting his wife's.

"And you just let them take it?" Joshua said, astonished. Joseph looked at the boy in anger and then retreated into grief.

"It is not so easy, Joshua," his father lamented.

"For some perhaps," Joshua said, retreating to his bed.

Mary walked over and placed hands on her husband's face and kissed him. "He's just a boy, he does not know any better," she said, looking over at Joshua's closed eyes.

"Mary, if He doesn't know any better then who is there to teach him? The boy could smite me with a thought."

Mary put her hand over her husband's lips. "Enough," she whispered, shaking her head. "He is not ready."

"I think he would disagree with you," Joseph moved his wife's hand away.

"He's a boy. All boys go through this phase," Mary argued.

"Most boys cannot turn a man into dust," Joseph said in a cautious whisper, looking over at the boy with his back turned to them. Mary followed his gaze, her muted expression turning to a grimace at the thought of her son hurting anyone.

↓ ↓ ↓ ↓ ↓ ↓

Joshua crept through the house, not making a sound, eyeing his mother and father with each cautious step as they slept until he finally reached the entrance to the hut. It was a warm night, and the stars lit up the sky. The stars were so bright, Joshua didn't even need a torch. Joshua was so confident he knew the way he could get there with his eyes closed. Learning the guards' routes had been easy. They were as predictable as cattle. They patrolled only certain areas and even the most serious of guards would sneak a break here and there. Getting to the old temple was an afterthought nowadays.

The old man was sitting at a table drawing something. Joshua tried to creep up on the old man but as always, right before he was about to touch the man on the shoulder, he was called out.

"I was caught off guard once. It won't happen again, I can assure you," the old man said, turning to face Joshua with a smile.

"But I did get close," Joshua said proudly.

The old man nodded. "You did. You did," he said, returning to his drawing.

"What is it? Your drawing..." Joshua leaned in to see and placed his hands on the table.

"I'm not sure exactly." The old man's hand continued to scribble back and forth.

The parchment had various scenes depicting a great war. The landscape was foreign to Joshua, with large, crumbled buildings and machines he had never seen. Men who looked like soldiers fought at a distance while beasts of all shapes and sizes infiltrated one side and fought beside the men.

"Is it a story?" Joshua asked, intrigued by what the pictures told.

"I'm sure it is to someone," the old man said, crumpling the parchment and tossing it into the fire.

"I wish I could draw like you." Joshua eyed the flames as they licked at the paper.

"Wishing can be dangerous," the old man said, handing Joshua the pen. "You can do anything you set your mind to." Joshua stared at the pen, twirling it in his hands. Joshua shrugged, placing the tip of the pen on his opposite hand and made little hash marks.

"Something is troubling you." The old man lifted Joshua's chin, so his gaze met his own.

"The Romans are starving us," the boy finally spat out what had been his reason for coming all along. The old man nodded and walked to the shelf where his parchment was stacked.

"So, why don't you make more food?" The old man said, placing the parchment down on the table in front of them. The boy was shaking his head before the old man could even finish.

"They would just take more. That's what they do. They take." Joshua gripped the pen tighter.

"You're tired of being the one who is taken from?" Joshua nodded.

"Then stop them," the old man said.

Joshua shook his head. "It's not our way."

"The Romans know that. They count on that even. You could free your people with a thought. Boil these men's blood!" The old man was getting excited.

Joshua smiled at the thought but shook his head.

"Oh, come now, imagine it—Joshua the Savior! Joshua the Messiah! Or even Joshua, King of the Jews!" The old man presented each title loudly and spread his hands out in display. Joshua laughed at each one but placed the pen down.

"I have to get back to bed," the boy said, waving goodnight to the old man as he slipped through the crack and up the staircase. The old man sat at his desk and began to draw. The fat round stick figure lay in what appeared to be a bed. Creatures of all manner surrounded the figure.

↓ ↓ ↓ ↓ ↓ ↓

Thescolus lay in his bed, sweating. The darkness crept in all around him, extinguishing the flames on the candles surrounding his bunk. Thescolus had been having awful dreams of late. They were unlike anything he had experienced before, almost like a sea of memories. Each horrible thing crashing into the next. His father spanking his bare ass raw as his hand morphed into a clawed talon. The other children in his village stomping on him as they laughed and spit. Piss trickled down his throat as the boys' cocks unleashed hot, painful streams. Their cocks were growing teeth and then mouths as they joined in on the laughing. The cacophony of laughs hurt his head as he tried to cover his ears.

The boys morphed into the Jews he was tasked with collecting from. Their laughter grew louder until he couldn't take it any longer and he lashed out.

He screamed as the pain in his hand woke him abruptly. He had punched the wall so hard that his hand felt like it had shattered.

"Fuck!" Thescolus said, wrapping his hand with his standard. The golden eagle of his legion turned crimson, making the bird look like it had mauled some rabbit to shreds. The sun was already rising as the roosters crowed, welcoming this already disastrous day. He would get dressed, clean his hand and collect the remaining rations, trying to put those horrible dreams out of his head. Thescolus looked down at his hand. It was swelling and he could feel his heartbeat throughout it. Each beat echoing a throb of pain, making the soldier wince. He thought of the Jews and their laughter and how they had hurt him. Dream or no dream.

☩ ☩ ☩ ☩ ☩ ☩

Markus was already regretting drinking what little wine he had left. He was not proud of it and he knew his mother and father would look down on such things, but the drink made him forget. It reminded him of a time before the Romans, when he and his friends were free to do and say as they pleased. A time when he did not need to surrender his grain and wine to soldiers who mocked him and his God. The dreams of late, however, were only more of a reason to hide as deep as he could in the bottle. His back would ache at first and he would fall to the ground, spilling the stones for the new temple. The Roman, his features melting into a mess of exposed bone and teeth, shouted for him to get up, spraying pieces of his melted flesh with each command. Markus could not rise though in the dream and so the Roman was on him in an instant.

His whip tore into the back of Markus's neck and back. The skin erupted with each crack, bursting his flesh open like an overripe fruit. The pain was excruciating, but the fear was worse as fingers spread wide from the wounds on his back, stretching the skin further, exposing his muscles in a wet glistening display of flesh until his skin was completely ripped from his body. Markus always woke up screaming, his back burning and aching from the scratches he had dug into himself.

↓ ↓ ↓ ↓ ↓ ↓

The morning started off uneventfully for Thescolus, with each of the men going about their duties. Stone was being laid, crops were harvested and business went about as usual. Thescolus was trying to calm himself down. The images from his dreams kept flashing through his head, reigniting the anger inside him. These Jews hated him, they hated his culture, and his authority over them. He knew it would only be a matter of time before one of these ungrateful bastards tried to take him and his fellow soldiers out. He saw how they all looked at him. The disdain, the hatred, the disrespect. A legionnaire broke his chain of thought as he walked up beside him and offered Thescolus a bite of his apple, which he declined.

"Ever think about what they think of us?" the soldier asked, taking a bite out of his apple. Thescolus looked over at the man, not recognizing him, and turned his gaze back on the Jews.

"They hate us," Thescolus said, leaving nothing up for debate. The soldier nodded.

"Someone should show them they should respect us. Realize that they are privileged to be part of our empire," the soldier said, taking another giant bite from the apple, causing the juice to dribble down his chin.

Markus was breathing hard. The stones seemed heavier than usual, but most of his fellow workers seemed to be having no trouble at all. He wondered if his lack of sleep was making him weak or his muscles more tired. The Romans kept staring at him with smirks and half-assed grins. They were mocking him and his work, or lack thereof. He could feel their stares boring into him. These Pagans would keep taking until none of his culture or his people were left. A fellow worker broke his train of thought as the man crunched into a bright green apple.

"If they see you eating that they will whip you," Markus said, pointing to the apple. The man split the apple in two, to Markus's amazement, and offered him half.

"Guess we should finish it quickly then, brother," the man said. Markus looked at the guards who, for the first time since he had walked on to the fields, were not looking his way. Markus took the apple and nodded in appreciation, biting into the fruit. The juices were sweet with a little sour that made his mouth pucker. The feeling quickly dissipated and the juices from the apple cleansed his dry mouth. Markus and the man finished the apple in three crisp bites, nodding at each other in enjoyment.

"Think the Romans care what we think of them?" The man said, leaning on his shovel. Markus was shaking his head before the man even finished.

"They don't care, they never have, never will." Markus dug his shovel into the dirt. The man nodded and started to dig as well.

"Someone should make them care. Make them realize they are lucky to be among His chosen people."

Markus looked over at the Romans, their features seemed to shift with each movement. One soldier's face was a normal, plain looking man one second and a mask of bone and teeth the next. Markus wiped the nervous sweat away from his brow and shook the image out of his head.

"We should show them we don't belong under anyone's boot," the man said, driving his shovel over and over into the dirt.

Markus could hear the soil, like the man was digging inside his skull. The pounding and tearing of the dirt made Markus furious and annoyed.

"Show them we are tired of the whip."

Markus's back erupted into pulses of agony. He could feel the hands moving his muscles aside, trying to reach out through his skin. He desperately tried to reach behind him but he couldn't quite reach and so he ran, hoping that somehow, he could outrun the pain.

The soldier took loud bites, each one echoing inside Thescolus' head, causing flashes of his dream. Each chomp of the apple was a kick or a punch from a Jew. He finally had to walk away from the soldier and his chewing, otherwise he felt his head would explode. The pain was blinding. Each chomp was a cacophony of Hebrew curses and laughs thrown his way. Each prayer to their false God rang through his head like a cock crowing inside his skull. Thescolus' body betrayed him and he vomited right at the moment a Jew was rounding the corner.

Markus' eyes stung. The thick viscous fluid that filled them was warm and sour smelling. He rubbed at his eyes with his hands, finally giving up and using his garment to rub his eyes clean, or at least not filled with vomit. As Markus's vision cleared, he saw the Roman wiping his mouth and standing taller.

"Get back to work Jew," the Roman ordered, wiping his mouth again with a bloody wrapped hand. Markus didn't move, though. The Roman's face was flickering between skin and bone so fast it reminded him of some type of grotesque hummingbird.

"I said get back to work!" the Roman cried as he slapped Marcus across the face with the back of his hand.

Show them, a voice echoed in Markus' head as he fell to the floor.

Show them, a voice throbbed in Thescolus' skull as he drew his blade.

Markus grasped at the loose dirt and tossed it into the soldier's eyes, making him stagger and swing his sword wide, missing its intended target. Thescolus went for another swing of his gladius, but the blade was stuck in something. He turned his gaze to follow the shaft of his arm up to the hilt of the blade that was stuck firmly into the skull of an elderly Jew woman. Her hands were shaking, dropping the bundle of blankets she had been carrying. Her mouth was puckering, babbling sounds like a child trying to sound out a word. Horror overtook Thescolus for only a moment at the realization of his mistake, then he heard the voice again.

Show them. He placed his foot on the old woman's chest and pulled the blade free with a scrraa-pppp sound and turned to find Markus's eyes wide and full of anger. He felt the rock push the top part of his helmet down and into his flesh and skull. Thescolus' vision in his left eye went dark and his balance wavered, making him roll back on his heels. Markus rushed forward, driving his shoulder into the man and sending them both tumbling into the street. Thescolus used the momentum of the roll to send Markus up and over, landing in the muddy soil the men had been working on. The Jews were crowding around now, shocked at the violence playing out before them.

"Get back!" Thescolus ordered, pointing his blade toward the onlookers. Markus drove his teeth into the man's ankle and arched back, causing Thescolus to roar in pain as muscle slowly separated from bone, flesh, and tendon and stretched until it snapped in Markus's animal like bite. Thescolus crumbled to the ground and reached down, feeling a bloody fountain of gore where his ankle should be. Markus licked his lips and hocked the bloody spit onto the crying Roman. The thunder of boots and shields echoed all around as a wall of legionnaires were heading Markus's way. He hopped over the Roman and grabbed his sword, rising quickly to address the men in the gathered crowd.

"We need to show them that this is our home! That they cannot come into our temples and our lands without the wrath of God's people!"

A few of the men cheered while others hurried their loved ones away. The remaining men grabbed their shovels and formed a line with Markus, the Roman crying out in pain, laid before them.

Joshua heard the rattling of the Romans' armor as they marched past his hut. He looked into his parents' bedroom, but it was empty, causing panic to run down his spine. He rushed outside and followed the Romans as closely as he could without drawing attention. The Romans stopped and pointed their spears toward a group of Jews armed with shovels and one sword while a Roman soldier cried out in pain.

"YOU WILL DISPERSE NOW!" the commander of the soldiers ordered, putting emphasis on the word now. The Jews looked nervous, but the leader of the group placed the sword at the back of the Roman's neck on the ground.

"YOU WILL DISPERSE!" The man countered, pushing the tip of the blade in slowly, causing cries of pain from the injured Roman.

"I say we kill them all!" one of the soldiers yelled, drawing grunts from the rest.

"Quiet! Hold the line!" the commander shouted, trying to find where the unruly soldier was. Joshua saw the soldiers mumbling and shifting around like they were uncomfortable. He could feel something in the wind, like the rain right before a thunderstorm. The entire world seemed to slow to a crawl for only a second, but in that moment Joshua saw the old man from the temple whispering into the soldier's ears. He moved between the men in an instant. Each blink of Joshua's eyes had the old man speaking into the ear of another soldier or another of the opposing Jews.

Joshua and the old man's eyes met for the briefest of moments, and then one of the Jews threw a stone. Joshua saw it all unfold before him in what must have been under a minute, but to the boy it felt like hours. The Roman who had been hit with the rock charged forward, his spear tip digging into a man's stomach and lifting him off his feet, and throwing him down hard into the mud. Markus, the leader of the group, drove his sword through the Roman's neck, severing it from his body. This led the commander of the Romans to order the charge. The Romans' spears lunged forward into the group of men. Some were skewered, while the rest, including Markus, battered the spears away and counter rushed into the soldiers. Markus leveraged his armpit over one of the soldier's shields arcing the swing of his sword right across the soldier's neck causing the soldier's head to fall unnaturally to the right until the blade struck the man's spine sending a sickening shiver up Markus's arm.

Joshua was horrified at the chaos before him. One Roman drove his shield down, dislocating a man's jaw and crushing through the back of the man's skull. Spears pierced one man from all sides, turning him into a human pincushion. The triangle spear tips ripped the flesh from his muscles, spraying the ground with gobs of crimson muck. The man stumbled toward Joshua, trying to stop the blood from one of the various holes until falling down to his knees and then across Joshua's feet.

"Stop." Joshua tried to speak, but the words wouldn't come out. Two men held one Roman by the arms while the man with the sword drove it deep into his chest. The remaining soldiers quickly skewered through the men with precise armed strokes, each thrust aimed right through the heart.

"Stop," Joshua whispered. The words crawled up his throat and out of his mouth in less than a whimper. The leader of the men backed away, waving his sword at the soldiers in wild desperation. The legion commander walked behind the soldiers looking for any Jews still breathing, moaning, or showing any sign of life. Instead of getting them aid like Joshua had hoped, he casually drove the tip of his sword into each one of them.

"Stop," Josh uttered, the words finally escaping his lips loud enough for the commander to hear him.

Thunk. The ring of the blade echoed in Joshua's head.

"Stop."

Thunk.

"STOP!"

THUNK.

"I said...STOP!"

The force of the words escaped Joshua's lips like a wave, encompassing both soldier and Jew alike. The men froze in terror as their skin pulsed, expanding in and out like a grotesque bullfrog. Joshua's anger was pulsing out of him, intensifying with each glance at the dead men on the ground. The pulsing intensified throughout each of the men's bodies, stretching the skin to the point of ripping. Blood started to pour from the men's eyes, ears, nose, and mouth like a dam had burst that had been holding back death. Each blood filled sack ruptured sending gallons of blood and puss rushing towards Joshua's feet. The warm sticky liquid woke Joshua from his trance, striking him with horror at what he had done to his own people and the Romans. Joshua rushed to the leader of the men and cradled his head, trying hard to avoid the open, loose blister the left side of his face had become.

"I'm...I'm so sorry my brother," Joshua stuttered, trying to fight back the tears flowing from his face.

"Wha...what are you?" the man asked, terrified.

Joshua didn't know how to answer him.

"What's your name?" Joshua asked, trying to avoid the question.

"Markus," the man said, letting his fear go for some reason. He felt a strong sense of calm, and all his pain was dissipating. Joshua rubbed his hand over the man's forehead and kissed it. Love and compassion flowed out of Joshua now, just as easily as the rage had.

"I was so angry," Markus said, not struggling with the pain any longer.

"I know. I was also. It is dangerous. It's a seed that grows rapidly and poisons anyone around it. It consumes us so easily that we don't see our own destruction..." Joshua looked at the corpses all around him.

"Or those around us." Joshua looked down in shame. Markus lifted his hand, caressing Joshua's cheek.

"I forgive you," Markus said with a smile spreading across his bloody lips as his head fell back in death. Joshua's mouth hung open. He felt powerless, grateful, hurt and, above all, angry. He took in several deep breaths, calming himself, focusing on his surroundings. The Romans couldn't find out about this, it would only cause more suffering for his people.

The bodies around Joshua started to age rapidly. Hair grayed and then fell out, eyes clouded and melted, skin and bone sank deep into the soil. The Romans' armor turned back into the minerals they had started as and slithered down into the earth, leaving no trace of anyone. Joshua rose to his feet, looking for the old man, but he was gone. He looked at the soil and was confident nobody would notice. He looked out across the field toward the old temple and started walking.

↓ ↓ ↓ ↓ ↓ ↓

"OLD MAN!" Joshua's screams echoed throughout the old temple like a soundboard, his cries yelling back at him in response. The old man kept drawing on his parchment, not paying any attention to Joshua or his cries.

"OLD MAN!" Joshua cried through the opening and down the staircase.

"Evening, young Joshua," the old man replied, still not looking back.

"Why don't I know your name? Or where you came from? I keep trying to think back on the day we met, and it escapes me. Why is that?" Joshua asked, standing a few feet behind the old man.

"Old men are often unremarkable and not worth remembering, I suppose," the old man chuckled.

"What. Is. Your. Name?" Joshua commanded.

"I don't know yet. I'm growing tired of the old ones, to be quite honest." The old man sounded annoyed.

Joshua grabbed the old man by the shoulder and turned him around to face him, only to have the man's robe fall to the ground like he had never existed. Gusts of wind erupted from all corners of the cave. Joshua couldn't keep up with the movement.

"Are you looking to leave me in the ground as well, Joshua?" The old man's voice was different now—darker and angrier.

"I didn't know what I was doing! I didn't mean to..."

"You did exactly what you meant to, and you did it well, Joshua." The old man's voice echoed all around.

"That's not what I wanted. I never want to feel like that again. I don't want anyone to feel like that again!" Joshua cried.

"They have been doomed since the beginning, Joshua. Nothing you do can change what they are," the voice proclaimed.

"You could have been helping them! You could have been teaching them a different way!" Joshua screamed at all four corners of the temple.

"A different way?" the voice asked, amused. The laughter that echoed throughout the temple had Joshua covering his ears in pain. The wind blew furiously throughout the temple, each gust of wind carried a deafening laugh until it was gone. Joshua looked at the parchment strewn about the temple floor. Some depicted acts of the cruelest debauchery, while others depicted an owl in mid-flight. The one Joshua bent down to hold in his hands depicted a king atop a throne of infant corpses and a bright star off in the background.

Chapter 7
The Darkness Now Seems Normal

Dan's head was reeling from what he just heard. He didn't know why but he felt in his bones the voice was telling the truth, but he couldn't accept that.

"Blasphemy," Dan said, foolishly hoping the voice wouldn't push the subject further.

"Just because something upsets you, Dan, that doesn't make it untrue."

"Then why wasn't that in the gospels? Why is there no mention of that story at all?" Dan asked.

"Just the gospels? Or the other sixty something books, Dan?"

Dan knew about the "missing" or "lost" books of the bible. They went over them in seminary school.

"That story is in none of those,"

"Have you ever read them?"

"No, but a story like that surely would have been mentioned."

"There is only one written copy of that story and that book has indeed been lost, Dan."

"Convenient," Dan said, satisfied he had dodged this debate.

"No, Dan, more like Covenant," the voice countered.

Dan didn't answer, forgetting that his confused expression couldn't be seen through the small partition.

"Covenant. It's a simple word. It appears twenty times in your King James. Testament, however, only appears thirteen times," the voice said like it should all make sense.

"I'm not a Rabbi. I don't know if you noticed the dead guy hanging on the cross when you walked in?"

The voice chuckled. "I'm breaking down your walls. That's good, Dan."

Dan didn't argue. If you can't beat them, join them, came to mind.

"The word is the same in Hebrew. It is up to the writer which to choose and thus one sentence could mean something else entirely."

"That is far different than leaving out an entire book about Jesus melting a bunch of men...just in my professional opinion," Dan laughed.

"Just pointing out inconsistencies, Dan."

The words hit Dan hard with a feeling of nostalgia. In seminary school, Dan had always been the thorn in his teacher's side. *Why* had always seemed to be Dan's answer to every question.

"When I was in school, I used to question things..." Dan began.

"I thought this was m*y* confession, Dan?"

"Just shut up and listen."

↓ ↓ ↓ ↓ ↓ ↓

Dan's first day of class was starting in five minutes. In five minutes, there would be no going back. Two cigarettes. That's all. Two cigarettes left to be a sinner. Dan dropped the butt from his lips and lit up another one. The priest and other seminarians passed his way, avoiding the smoke with waves of their hands. Dan blew the smoke out of his mouth and back into his nostrils. He watched the door close behind the last of the students and then looked up toward the sky.

"You sure about this?" Dan asked, holding his arms out in surrender. But after a moment, nothing came of it and so, with a reluctant sigh, he took one final deep inhale and headed for the door. The room was lined with dull looking people, none of whom showed any interest in Dan's abrupt opening of the doors. These men were all writing down the scripture on the board.

For we are God's handiwork, created in Christ Jesus to do good works which God prepared in advance for us to do.

A bald man walked across the front of the class, reciting the verse loudly for all to hear.

"What does this verse mean to all of you?" the man asked. One student's hand shot up immediately.

"There's always fucking one," Dan said under his breath.

"I believe it means that we are all born good. The devil can influence us in many ways, but we are born with a plan for good that we can be swayed from."

"So, you're not sure?" The bald man kept pacing.

"I...um..."

"What is your name, son?"

"Matthew."

"Continue, Matthew," the bald man bid.

"It's my interpretation." Matthew shrugged.

"Your interpretation is what your flock will cling to, live their lives on. Let me be clear gentleman, for all of your congregations, you might as well be the pope or even God himself."

The classroom shifted around in their seats, looking to each other for guidance on how to act in the situation.

The bald man stopped and smiled, looking at each one of his students. He nodded toward Dan, who was the only one smiling. "Blasphemy, I know, I know," he said, trying to lighten the mood.

"No, I am not the devil in disguise. My name is Father Mason and I will be teaching you how to believe in what you're saying."

The boys all looked uncomfortable for the second time since entering the room, except for Dan.

Matthew raised his hand. "Father, I'm not so sure I understand. We are all men of faith. I mean, why would we be here if we weren't?"

"Matthew, you may think you believe. You may have read your bible and had heated debates before, but you can only be an agent of God if you believe one hundred percent in what you are preaching."

Dan didn't bother raising his hand. "Isn't the bible all interpretation?"

"Your name, son?"

"Dan."

"Dan, the bible is the word of God. It is what we hold true according to the Holy Mother Church. Who are you to question his word?" Father Mason asked.

"Just a man," Dan said.

"Aw, now you're getting it, Dan. You see, every one of you will be attacked with logic, with science, and those two things can only be defeated with one simple thing. Anyone care to answer?"

The room was hooked on Father Mason's every word now, but didn't dare answer.

"Faith, gentleman. It is the ultimate weapon that you wield while wearing that collar. Men and women will come to you on Sunday and ask you to help them. To explain all the shitty horrible things in their lives and you will have some answers, but more often than not you will be left out in the cold among the wolves, and all you will have to fight them off is this," Father Mason said, taking a finger and poking the bible on the lector before him.

"Can we have an example?" Dan asked, his curiosity piqued now.

"A couple of years ago, I had a man come to confession. He was distraught, and had been drinking. He had blocked the partition with something. He told me nobody could know who he was because of what he had done. He begged me not to tell anyone. Told me that he had truly given himself over to Christ and he thought about ending his life daily for what he had done. I assured him that his confession was between him and the Lord and I was bound to hear it."

Father Mason looked the class over, taking a mental headcount of the nods in agreement.

"He told me of his urges towards children."

The class shifted and fidgeted in the seats again.

"He had never acted on the urges, but it was getting tougher to control each day. He distanced himself from situations that would tempt him. Friends' birthday parties for their children, neighborhood

BBQs, but of course, people had children, and it was inevitable."

Dan was starting to get nervous. These stories never ended well.

"One day, his coworker invited him over for dinner and, since he was looking for a promotion, he accepted. On his way back from the bathroom upstairs, he saw his coworker's son changing in his bedroom. He stopped a little too long, and the boy noticed crying out for his parents. The man, scared that the boy would alert his parents, covered the boy's mouth and placed his knees on his chest while trying to think of a plan. He said it must have only been ten seconds. Ten seconds was all it took to suffocate the boy."

The classroom of men were wiping sweat from their faces and unbuttoning their collars, the priest equivalent of what the fuck.

"He placed one of the boy's belts around his neck and placed him in the closet. He told me it was the first time he had ever prayed. The police came and said no investigation was needed. It was an obvious case of suicide even though the parents had said he showed no sign of depression, no behavioral problems. But such is the way of our world."

Matthew raised his hand again. "Did you forgive him?"

"Should I have? What would you all have done?"

The men didn't look at each other this time, but within. Each man was running the scenario over in his mind.

"Show of hands how many of you would have not forgiven him? C'mon, be honest, you're not a priest yet."

About ten percent of the class raised their hands, some slower than others.

"How many of you would have forgiven him?"

The remainder of the class held their hands up, not sure if they should be ashamed or not.

All except Dan.

Father Mason raised an eyebrow. "Dan, time to get in the game or find a new sport. God doesn't allow us to sit on the sidelines."

Dan sat there for a moment, fighting the mixed emotions clashing inside his head. "How do I turn it off? Tell me how I'm supposed to give it over to God."

Father Mason nodded and walked over to Dan, placing his hand on his shoulder.

"You're not a judge, Dan. You're not a jury, and you are definitely not an executioner. All of those burdens are not ours, thankfully," he said to the rest of the class, drawing smiles and chuckles.

"Your job is simply to deliver forgiveness to those who seek it...even if you believe they don't deserve it."

Dan nodded and raised his hand.

✛ ✛ ✛ ✛ ✛ ✛

The next couple months flew by with Dan learning the usual teachings. He learned popular verses and how to turn them into sermons. How to grow his congregation using community focus and labor groups. The money aspect of it bugged him, but he learned quickly that working for the lord had to pay for him and his paycheck depended entirely on putting butts in the seats. At times, he would imagine how stupid he would look. Would he learn guitar like the popular Christian pastors he knew did? Unlikely, he didn't have a musical bone in body. Would he try using popular movies in his sermons to keep it lively? Dan grimaced at comparing Christ to fucking Iron Man.

He needed to come up with cash, and if he wasn't willing to do the gimmicky stuff, this was going to be a long, tough job. Dan often would walk off his troubles late into the night. He would only realize how far he had walked when a car or a siren would wake him to his unfamiliar surroundings. On this night, Dan realized he was not in the greatest of areas. The glances that came his way were not threatening. His collar bought him a certain clearance. Murder and mayhem were bad enough, but killing a man of God was a line most wouldn't dare cross. There was a club that released a purple smoke up ahead. When the doors opened, a couple of girls dressed in almost nothing were sharing a cigarette. Dan looked back at the way he came and then toward the two women. He lifted one leg in the air back toward home and then swung it around in the other direction and headed toward the girls.

"Holy shit!" One of the girls laughed, tapping her friend on the shoulder, pointing Dan's way.

"I assure you my shits are just as unholy as yours," Dan said, ripping his collar off and stuffing it into his pocket. The girl next to Dan took a long drag of the cigarette and offered it in Dan's direction. He took it and breathed in a long puff of smoke. The girl's lipstick had a taste of bubblegum to it, which made Dan roll his tongue over the cancer stick before handing it back to her.

"You really a priest?" the girl asked, taking the cigarette back.

"Not yet, still in school," Dan said, holding his hands up.

"Fuck, you got to go to school for that too?" The other girl laughed at this.

"I'm Dan," he said, extending his hand.

The girls took it and introduced themselves.

"I'm Max and this is Rhonda," the girl closest to Dan said.

Dan leaned in to whisper in her ear. "Max, don't you know it's bad to lie to a priest?"

"That so? Well, you let me know when you find one, ok preacher man?" Max said, turning and urging Rhonda towards the door.

"Our break is over. You coming in?"

Dan eyed the girls over. Each one seducing him with their body and a promise in their eye.

"No, no, I don't think I can," Dan said, defeated. The girls started to fondle each other, teasing each other's lips and feeling the other up, basking in Dan's frustration.

"Suit yourself, altar boy." The girls laughed as they stepped back into the cloud of smoke.

Dan walked home, fighting the erection in his pocket the whole way and praising himself for not giving into temptation.

↓ ↓ ↓ ↓ ↓ ↓

"May I interject?" The voice caught Dan off guard.

"If you must. I haven't interrupted you—I'd like to point out, though?"

"I think you're trying to confess something here. Trying to make me understand that you are a man who overcame all the temptations I supposedly threw your way?"

"No, What I'm trying to say is that I knew you had nothing to do with it. I sought it out, and it found me. I put myself in those situations and came out stronger for denying them."

"So you admit I don't control what you do?"

Dan thought for a moment, choosing his words with utmost care.

"No more than God does."

The voice started laughing, realizing what Dan was trying to say.

"Is that what you took from the saying on the board that day, Dan? That he tests you all the most? That you're better than the average person? Or maybe you're saying I can only tempt people like those women you wanted to fuck? You humans never change."

It was Dan's turn to laugh. "I'm saying that my job is to do exactly what the Lord asks of me. That I learned from a man smarter than I that God does not allow men like me to sit on the sidelines. I'm not better than anyone, but I am strong enough to shield myself while grabbing another's hand. You claim we don't change, but I had a man's wisdom change me and put me on a path to where I help people in the darkest of times."

"Ok, Dan. Continue please, no more interruptions. I give you my word."

↓ ↓ ↓ ↓ ↓ ↓

"I don't think I can continue coming to class," Dan said, wringing his hands as Father Mason stopped grading papers.

"Ok, why is that?" Father Mason asked, dropping his glasses atop the papers.

"I don't feel like I should be in charge of people's salvation."

"Well, Dan, luckily you are not. God is."

"You know what I mean," Dan said, not looking forward to the debate.

"What do I have to tell you to get through to you that someone's soul is not in your hands?"

"You told us we weren't a judge, but if I don't forgive them, I am damning them to Hell."

"Then that person would walk into the next confessional and be forgiven Dan." Father Mason said, rubbing between his eyes.

"Then what is the fucking point? If that's all it takes—if we are a revolving door of forgiveness—what stops them from acting like animals again?"

Father Mason breathed in, held it for a moment, and leaned back in his chair.

"You, Dan. You are what stops them. You teach them a better way and every time they fall, and they will fall Dan, you pick them up and you dust them off and you say do better. You're not a God Dan. You're a father. And every time your dumbass children touch the stove, even after you've told them they are going to burn their dumb little fingers, you blow on them and you bandage them up. And then you tell them you still love them because God loves them." Father Mason pointed to the ceiling.

Dan rubbed his face in frustration. "And what if they don't ever listen? What if they never change?" Dan was trying not to feel defeated.

"It's not their job to listen, Dan. That's the job that God chose for you."

↓ ↓ ↓ ↓ ↓ ↓

"Do you regret becoming a priest?" The voice asked, filled with curiosity.

Dan hesitated, but only for a moment.

"Sometimes. It's not easy hearing the same voices come in asking to be forgiven and then back the next week for the same thing," Dan admitted.

"Why do it then? What made you want to wear the cloth in the first place, Dan?"

↓ ↓ ↓ ↓ ↓ ↓

"I want to thank you all for coming. I know that Ramona would have appreciated all the love and support you all have shown me and my family in our time of mourning. My sons John and Dan are especially touched and thankful for all the cards and meals you all have dropped off. Lord knows I can't cook like Ramona, so the boys say keep the meals coming."

The church all chuckled, turning to look at the two boys seated in the front aisle. They both smiled uncomfortably at the hundreds of eyes that looked them up and down. Dan couldn't take it anymore, though. His skin was itching with the added pressure. He missed his mom. He looked at all the people with their sympathetic stares. It angered him. Where were all these people when his mother was sick? Where were the hugs and handshakes when his mom needed someone to watch them while she went to counseling? Or when he and his brother needed to be picked up from school when his mom had been rushed to the hospital? These fake people with their fake smiles and comfort. He opened the confessional, plopping down on the seat and leaning against the wall. Happy to be away from people, from his mom's corpse and his sadness.

"You're supposed to confess your sins."

The voice from the other side of the confessional startled Dan.

"Fuck!" Dan said, kicking the wall separating him and the priest on the other side.

"Good, there's one...got any others?" The voice asked, trying to make the boy laugh.

"No, now leave me alone." Dan turned away from the open partition.

"Sorry, kid, them's the rules. You can only be in here if you're a sinner or you're forgiving sins. So want to tell me what's bugging you?" the priest asked.

"My mom's dead," Dan replied, trying to sound like it didn't affect him at all.

"I'm sorry to hear that, my child. Did she know God before she left us?"

"No, he never came down to breakfast," Dan said mockingly.

"I meant, was she baptized?" The priest asked.

"No, mom wasn't very religious." Dan felt somewhat embarrassed given this present company.

"I see, and what about you?"

Dan thought for a moment. He believed in God. At least, he thought he did. Getting older made things fuzzy, like when his older schoolmates would tease him for believing in Santa. He still believed he just questioned it sometimes.

"I'm mad at him."

"Because he took your mom from you, yes?"

"Yes."

"What if I told you she wasn't in pain anymore? That he took her to be with him in heaven where she's waiting for you?"

"I would say you're a liar." Dan didn't hesitate.

"Is it lying if I believe it?"

Dan didn't know the answer to that in all honesty. He thought about his mom in heaven, happy and safe. It did seem better to think of her there and not in the box twenty feet away, rotting.

"She wasn't baptized." The worry crept into Dan's voice.

"It's not too late. If you want, you can stand in for her."

Dan thought for a moment, but only a moment.

"If I get baptized she can go to heaven?" Dan asked, wanting to hear a yes.

"That's correct. I am able to baptize you in her place and forgive her of all her sins, if that's what you would like."

Dan was nodding before the priest had finished.

"I'll do it," Dan answered immediately.

"It's an...outdated practice, but if it brings you peace, I don't see the issue with it. Your father would have to agree to it."

Panic filled Dan. His father was Catholic, but he had always been respectful of his mother's religious views. Having the ceremony in this church was tough enough, but as long as the rites were not expected and it was just a ceremony over the body, the church had allowed it.

"I'll make a deal with you." Dan was not sure if he would regret this decision.

"I'm not in the business of granting deals, son. I deliver salvation and forgiveness and that's all I can offer," the priest explained.

"I'll devote my life to the church. I'll trade you my soul for my mother's," Dan said, more confident now.

"My dear boy, that's not how it works."

"You have a choice. You can save two souls right now. My mother's and my own. I'll devote my life to the church and help people like you're helping me." Dan explained.

"Son, I understand..."

Dan interrupted him. "No, you don't understand. I am *angry*. I am hurt and I want to use it for something other than destruction, but right now, that's up to you. You can help me. Help my mother. Hell, even help the world by doing this one thing. Otherwise, I will turn from God and all his teachings. I will spread the word that he and his so-called priests abandon their flock when they are seeking to willingly join his people. So right now, right here, you either save two souls or you damn them."

The priest was silent in the little box. Dan could hear his own breathing as he waited for what seemed like years for any kind of sound. He thought of his mother twenty feet away in a box, much like the one he was in. Waiting to know whether both their souls would stay here—angry and choking for air—or be free, depended on this one holy man's actions. The door clicked open, and the priest walked to the other side of Dan's door. He knocked three times and waited for Dan to slide the cover open.

The priest looked defeated. Almost on the verge of tears when he looked into Dan's eyes and then back over at the group of people surrounding his mother's box. He turned back to Dan and looked upward, making the sign of the cross with his rosary. He lifted it over his head and placed it over Dan's, nodding to the boy.

"Your seminary starts Monday. Go grieve your mother."

↓ ↓ ↓ ↓ ↓ ↓

"Did your father ever find out?"

Dan let the question hang in the air for a long time until pulling himself away from the memory.

"Eventually. We didn't talk for a while after that, and my brother and I disagreed on things."

"Well, I hope you don't offer family counseling to your parish, Dan." The voice laughed and Dan couldn't help but crack a smile despite his best efforts.

"No, no, I stick to trying to save individual souls. Much easier that way." Dan mused.

"Isn't it though? How many do you think you have saved?" the voice asked in a genuine tone.

Dan thought for a moment, going over the people he had heard confess, and then quickly gave up realizing how impossible the task was. "If it was just one, then it was worth it," Dan said proudly.

"Jason Fone, middle-aged, divorced, couple of kids," the voice proclaimed.

Dan thought of the name, but it didn't ring any bells. "Confession is anonymous. If I'm supposed to recognize that name, I don't." Dan worried about where this was heading.

"Jason is boring, he goes to work, tries to be a good dad, and has zero impact on his community or the world, really."

Dan's stomach was tightening into knots.

"Jason also has somewhat of an online presence in the marketing community of cosplay. He is friends with the judges of conventions and has even voted on some himself."

Dan knew where this was going. It was a conversation that every priest had with themselves.

"Girls sometimes would message Jason asking for tips and guidance and of course he would offer his influence, but at a cost."

Dan was trying to not picture this Jason as some hovering figure. Something less than human.

"The cost, you see, were videos and pictures of the women hurting themselves. Inserting objects into places that didn't quite fit, Dan."

Dan was holding his breath, hoping that if he didn't breathe, the story couldn't find him somehow.

"Jason came to you one day, Dan, and asked you for forgiveness. You crossed your heart, made him say some Hail Marys, and Jason's soul was clean as a whistle."

"That's not how it works," Dan spit out, inhaling and exhaling, trying to keep his gasps from being heard.

"Yes, do tell me how you are not responsible for him doing this over and over because he knows he can always be forgiven."

"You have to *want* to be forgiven. God knows if you want forgiveness or not." Dan was getting defensive.

"But you don't, do you?" the voice accused.

"That's impossible to know. I can only go off of what they tell me."

"You can forgive someone's sins, though. What an interesting power God grants you, Dan."

"I'm getting tired of you mocking me."

"That's the sad thing about it, Dan. I'm not mocking you. I'm just pointing out how useless and insignificant your role is in the long run."

"You want to talk about insignificant? You lose in every story. Every mention of your name is in defeat. What's the point of being scared of someone who always loses?"

"Careful, Dan..."

"You're a joke. A Halloween costume at best. Kids are more scared of Jason and Michael Myers than the Devil." Dan tried to continue, but his mouth started salivating. His eyes poured tears and his stomach wretched, producing a thick viscous string of hair and human shit. Dan stared in horror as he pulled on the greasy shit covered strands like some hellish magician. Dan kept trying to expel the anaconda-like hair strand, but it was never ending. Bile would rise and fall back down into his stomach, unable to escape his shit clogged throat. Finally, with a sickening thwack, the coarse coil of hair plopped onto the floor. Dan gasped in rushes of air, causing him to cough and spit up a watery mixture of phlegm, bile, and shit.

"Holy Mother of God," Dan exclaimed, holding his throat and looking at the almost ten foot coil of hair on the ground. The coil started to move, circling in on itself like some hairy rattlesnake. Dan lifted his knees to his chest and pulled them in as tightly against himself as he could. The coil was climbing, bobbing back and forth, almost like it was sniffing the air for Dan's presence.

"Our Father, who art in heaven..." Dan started to say, but was cut off by a voice chittering in his head.

"In Heeeeeaaaavvveeennn annndd soo faarrr away," the voice hissed. The coil sprouted shit covered teeth all along its abdomen. Each little set of teeth chattered as the coil slithered around Dan's legs and then up his pant leg and up through his shirt. Dan tried to continue the prayer, but was frozen in fear. The teeth weren't hurting him but instead, nibbling him almost like a lover teasing his body. This and the smell made him vomit all over himself and the coil, which in response cocked its head back, then shot back down Dan's throat. Dan realized he was screaming. There was nothing in his throat. The coil and all the filth was gone, even the stench was gone. It was like he had imagined the entire ordeal.

"Wha...what...what's going on?" Dan asked, looking for any indication that he wasn't going insane.

"What is it about you humans? You claim to believe and then when proof of your belief appears, you suddenly all become skeptics," the voice on the other side of the door stated.

"That wasn't...that wasn't real?" Dan asked as much as he stated.

"Felt pretty real, didn't it, Dan? Smelt real as well."

"What are you?" Dan asked, still questioning what had just happened.

"No, Dan, we are past introductions. Time to get in the game, Dan! God does not let you sit on the sidelines, remember?" the voice yelled like some sort of aggressive little league parent.

"Can't be...you...you can't be him," Dan whispered to himself, trying to keep his head from spinning. The whole box shook like someone had run full force and kicked it.

"ENOUGH!" the voice roared, snapping Dan back to his current surroundings.

"How could I possibly forgive you?" Dan was at a genuine loss.

"The same way you do with everyone, you listen, and then absolve me," the voice was instructing now.

"You are responsible for so much. You are the enemy, the deceiver, the prince of lies! You are God's enemy!"

"I AM NOT HIS ENEMY! I defied him once! What do you sniveling sacks of meat do besides defy him? He gave you this amazing planet, and you have destroyed it! He gave you dominion over the beasts and you decimated them! You were a mistake. A cosmic fuck up that should have been nothing more than a passing toy! Your entire species is a divine midlife crisis at best!"

They both sat in silence for a long while, neither one even breathing.

"Do you want to know how I know your existence is a mistake?"

"No, I don't think I do," Dan said, shaking his head in exhaustion.

"Because you ruined him. Let me tell you when I realized he was lost, Dan."

"Will you end this, then?" Dan pleaded.

"Only you can end this. Now listen."

↓ ↓ ↓ ↓ ↓ ↓

He was hungry. He couldn't deny it. Fasting was ninety percent mental, ten percent physical. Keeping the pain at bay was getting harder, but his thinking had become clearer after the moments of haziness and lethargy. The vultures had been following him for days now. Their circling helped him pass the time between meditation and thoughts on what his message would be. His father had been silent for days and however much it had frustrated him, he understood He answered when it was needed, even if he couldn't see it.

This would be fundamental to his message. God is in all things, even the bad. It would be up to his followers to find him and find comfort in that. This hurt him when he was younger. God seemed to be nowhere when needed. It had taken many years and an open mind to see that he was in the smallest of actions. When someone stood up for what they believed to be right, God was the one stoking the fire of courage within. When a birth had gone bad, God was in the community that rallied around the grieving parents. This would be the core of his teachings. God is in all of them and they need to believe in themselves and each other.

It would be the greatest test they would ever face, but he had faith in them. He had to—if what had been revealed to him in this palace of sand was true. His life would be lived for others and so, in his death, it would be the same. His stomach ached at the thought of it. The spot under his ribs pulsed with each heartbeat like some monk ringing a bell in his tower of flesh. He breathed in deep trying to push the fear and hunger out of his mind. The vultures cried, stirring him from his concentration. One of the buzzards was diving fast toward something rolling down the hill opposite of where Joshua sat. He narrowed his vision and noticed it was a spider. Its body tumbling down the sand like a ball. The vulture thought it would be an easy meal, but much to Joshua, and to the vulture's surprise, the spider launched itself onto the vulture's neck, causing the bird to crash headfirst into the sand. The crack was so loud it echoed in the silence. The spider crawled its way inside the hole in the vulture's neck where its bone had severed the skin. Moments later, the bird convulsed, stretching and breaking like a cocoon of gore and feathers. The tiny spider's limbs morphed into that of a pale man and the feathers now resembled a long coat around the man making his way toward Joshua. The man tapped his forehead and draped an arm out wide in a greeting. Joshua nodded but kept seated. The man crossed his legs and plopped down in the sand and stared into Joshua's eyes. His hair was blond but dirty, while his face was incredibly unblemished, as if he had just come from the womb. On his belt, a tiny skull of what Joshua thought was a bat hung.

"You look much younger than I remember," Joshua stated, giving a hint of a smile. The man returned the grin and nodded.

"And you look much older than I remember, Joshua. When did you know it was me?" The man asked.

"Not long after you left, I looked over your drawings and asked my mother what they could possibly mean. They told me everything," Joshua said.

"Everything?" The man let the question hang in the air.

"Everything." Joshua nodded.

"Do tell me how that felt," the man said, leaning in like an excited child.

"That's why you come here? To visit and hear stories?"

"I love stories, Joshua. I even enjoy dreams contrary to what some may think."

"My mother was apprehensive at first. Joseph had looked like a weight had been lifted from his shoulders. I didn't understand where all this power had come from. I thought you were teaching me the ways of the old, like Solomon, even though it was forbidden. I learned through my mother that my gifts are from my father," Joshua explained.

"That must have been something to hear. To be the son of God, the Messiah, and not little Joshua who knew some magic tricks, eh?" The man smiled.

"It was indeed humbling." Joshua smiled.

"And what did you do with this knowledge? Did you clear the Romans Joshua? Or perhaps you lead your people to a place where they can be safe?" The man was trying to bait him.

"I reflected," Joshua replied, not taking the bait. The man scoffed and looked over his shoulders.

"You have done nothing. Do you think I haven't been watching? The Romans still rule your people. Your own call you a false prophet to the point where your cousin is looking more and more impressive. Talk about not living up to your potential, Joshua." The man shook his head, ending with a tsk-tsk sound.

"I disagree," Joshua said plainly and nothing more. The man shifted in his seat, grabbing a handful of sand while lifting his hand out before Joshua. The grains of sand turned midair into beans and back into sand before they hit the ground.

"You must be hungry," the man said, continuing his transformation over and over.

"I have all I need," Joshua replied, staring into the man's eyes and paying no attention to the food.

"Do you still know the magic I taught you?" The man cocked an eyebrow in curiosity.

"I have cleansed all teachings from you." Joshua's smile faded away.

"Powerless then? Yet I hear of miracles? Tell me then, Joshua, have you become a magician? Performing miracles by the sleight of your hand?"

Joshua breathed in. He was so thin his ribs looked like they were trying to reach through his skin.

The man's mouth opened, exposing a bright green apple in between his teeth. He took a loud bite, the crunch sounding like an explosion in Joshua's ears. He held it out for Joshua to take, but he did not move. The man looked at the apple, examining where his perfect teeth had ripped its flesh like a wolf tearing open a belly. He nodded and produced another apple and when Joshua ignored his second offer, a third popped out of the man's mouth and followed the other two in a circle while the man began to juggle.

"I forgot he's picky about these, isn't he?" the man said, leading his gaze to the fruit and then back at Joshua.

"Why did you teach me back then? Was it corruption? Jealousy? I often wonder." There was no anger in his voice. He simply wanted to know. The man stopped juggling, letting the apples fall thud, thud, thud, until the skin peeled back, and the meat of the fruit shriveled, dissolving back into sand.

"What is a man, Joshua? What separates man and beast?" This was meant to be rhetorical.

"Free will," Joshua tried to reply but was interrupted.

"Ah, ah, see, but is a man truly free? If you give a man two choices, of course he has the freedom to choose which one, but he is still shackled by those two choices, is he not?"

Joshua didn't answer, but he was listening.

"If a man has power, genuine power to change things, he then ceases to be a man because he is no longer shackled by circumstance. There is no true choice when you are forced to choose in the first place. I heard talk of a boy. A boy that would lead his people and all of man to Father's forgiveness. At first, I didn't believe the rumors or the whispers, but eventually one of my agents told me of a king and his fear of infants."

Joshua perked up at the mention of King Herod. The old man's drawing had sent him down a rabbit hole of pain and confusion, which he had never honestly been able to climb out of.

"I am well aware of the price others paid so that I may live," Joshua said solemnly.

"As you should, it's important to know whose blood is on one's hands." The man moved his hands one over the other in a washing motion.

"Did he tell you that it was part of a bigger picture? Or some grand plan?"

"He doesn't tell me anything. We don't talk often." Joshua looked almost disappointed.

"Don't take it personally. He seems to get bored easily." The man smiled, and they both shared a chuckle.

"Do you ever think he will abandon them? Admit that he was wrong about...this?" The man held his arms out indicating in all directions.

"I know he won't, and he has never been wrong about them," Joshua said, shaking his head.

"How can you be so sure?"

"Because I won't abandon them. They stumble and then fall, but more often than not, they surprise me." Joshua smiled.

"Ingenuity in ways of destruction. I agree they surprise even me, but why try to teach them again? How many chances do they get, Joshua? I tried to teach you when you were younger. I tried to show you a way that might have worked for them, but you turned away from it the second things got messy. They need to be taught a lesson. They need to know who they should bow to."

The man stopped, noticing Joshua drawing circles in the sand and smiling.

"Am I amusing you?" the man asked, annoyed.

"You sound like him. You two are more alike than either of you will ever admit."

The man had never been speechless. This made Joshua laugh out loud despite his efforts.

"He'll abandon you just like he abandoned me and at the end of it all, Joshua, you will disappoint him. Come with me. Teach them what they need to survive this life he has forced upon them and maybe we can save them."

Joshua shook his head. "They don't need what you are willing to teach. They were an idea once. A perfect idea that was so simple that it could not be more complex. Before the garden, before everything—they were love. That is what they need."

"Then what were we? Hmm? What was I if not perfect?"

"The example," Joshua said, sounding almost defeated. He reached out, almost touching the man's shoulder, but he pulled it away out of Joshua's reach.

"There will be a time, Joshua, when you need him. When you are at your lowest, and the world around you seems cold and painful. You will be down in that cave, and he will not answer you."

Joshua couldn't tell if the man was being figurative or not but could tell the man was speaking from experience.

"Last chance. I won't help you when the time comes," the man said, extending his hand.

"If you are not willing to offer help all the time, then you are missing the point," Joshua said, closing his eyes and resting his hands on his knees. The man stood, staring at Joshua for a long time until he finally retrieved his hand and disappeared. Joshua awoke from his meditation to the sound of babies crying all around him. It was cold all around him. The sand was soft with moisture from the air as the rain gave way to thunder. A crack of the thunder rang in Joshua's ears. Each bolt made the sound of an infant shrieking in pain and fear. The lightning struck the sand, sending a splash of crystalline glass.

All around Joshua, strike after strike of lightning made a river of glass. The cries turned to shrieks as the glass moved in on itself, forming into a mixture of sand, glass, and blood. The first infant's growl made Joshua cover his ears as its grotesque features came into form. Joshua noticed that there were six in total, all inching toward him, their jagged bodies and hands contorting in a quick terrible burst. Joshua reached out toward one of the children, trying to get a sense of what this creature was and maybe some way to help it, but it was no use. And just as quickly as he had extended his hand, it was cut by the swipe of the child's hand.

Joshua tried to keep his distance, but the sand was cumbersome, and the children were much faster than him in his starved and exhausted state.

"I can make them stop. All you need to do is ask," a voice soothed Joshua's sore ears, but he shook it from his mind. His right calf was sliced in his moment of distraction and he fell back, rolling down the hill.

"He's abandoned you here, alone, hungry, and now surrounded by enemies of his own making."

Joshua looked up to the skies, his vision blurred from the fall. Was he alone? Was he just another thing his father would grow tired of? The infants fell down the hill, stumbling like newly born deer on ice. Joshua's wound was flowing, making the sand around him turn into a clay-like substance. He smiled and looked towards the sky.

"In all things." Joshua laughed as he lifted his hand over the tiny blood pool. The blood began to spread through the ground like roots beneath a tree, branching out in all directions. The sand became a thick viscous paste. The infants stumbled into the muck toward Joshua, showing no regard for their own safety. The infants sank deeper into the congealed pool with each labored step. Joshua watched as some of the infants broke their limbs clean off, trying to advance in the thick, unforgiving muck. Joshua lifted his hand, causing the ground to solidify into a frozen lake of bloody red clay.

The infants all shrieked as the ground shattered, entombing their fragile bodies in the ancient sands. Joshua tightened the wrap around his wounds and started walking with a new determination.

↓ ↓ ↓ ↓ ↓ ↓

"I don't understand." Dan was trying to be more cautious about how he spoke now.

"None of you ever did," the voice quipped.

"Why attack him? I mean...It sounds almost like...you like him?"

"I told you before, I had no problem with him, Dan. Have you not been listening?"

"But then why?"

"To show him that whatever help or love he expects from our father is wildly misplaced."

"You...you wanted him to choose you."

"Now you're getting it, Dan."

"You showed him some magic tricks and left him some drawings and you thought he would...what? Look up to you? Call you dad?" Dan almost laughed.

"You are very close to having my pet come out of your asshole instead of your mouth, Dan," the voice threatened.

"Look, you want me to sit here and listen and forgive you, right? I can't do that if I'm terrified of saying the wrong thing."

THE MORNINGSTAR CONFESSION

The voice didn't answer right away, but Dan felt a little calmer.

"Fine, but tread carefully, Dan," the voice warned.

"If you wanted him to look up to you or join you or whatever, then why abandon him after his...incident?" Dan asked, trying not to point out the painful deaths his Lord and savior had supposedly committed. The mere fact he was trying to not point it out made the whole thing seem even more absurd.

"He was angry. I know all too well what being angry at someone you look up to can do. I needed to give him space to realize he was being lied to."

"I wouldn't say lied to..." Dan mused.

"That's precisely what they did to him up until the end, Dan."

"They were hiding him. Protecting him."

"He didn't need protection. With a mere thought, he could have made anyone who aimed to harm him cease to exist. They wanted him to obey them. I know how that feels."

"They were protecting their child from persecution. You had to train him by your own account. What would an infant be able to do? Parents are meant to protect their children."

"Is that so, Dan?"

Dan nodded, even though he couldn't be seen.

"You would protect him, would you? If only you had been so protective back when it mattered."

Dan's stomach dropped through the floor. There was no way he could have known about that. Only two other people in the world knew about that.

↓ ↓ ↓ ↓ ↓ ↓

"Why do we always have to meet in this shithole?" Max asked, adding more sugar to her cup of coffee.

"Good pancakes and nobody bothers us here," Dan said, taking the plate of pancakes from the waitress.

"Nobody bothers you, you mean," Max said, taking a sip of her coffee and adding even more sugar. Dan breathed in deep and exhaled as he cut into the pancakes with exaggerated force.

"Do you want to spend time together or not?" Dan said with a mouth full of syrupy cake. They'd had this conversation too many times.

"You know I do. I'm just tired of being something you hide." Max moved her coffee cup to the side in defeat.

"I don't hide you. I mean, I don't want to." Dan lifted his hands in surrender.

"Then don't. Quit. Do something else." Max slid her hands across the table, palms up, until Dan placed his on top.

"You know I can't do that," Dan said, holding her hands tight. He knew she would pull them away like she always did.

"Can't? Or won't?" Max pulled her hands away and folded her arms and looked out the diner window. Dan rubbed his forehead and let his fist drop hard on the table, shaking the silverware and making Max jump.

"I hate when you do that. How many fucking times have I told you not to do that? For a priest, you're a pretty shitty listener, ya know that?"

The waitress dropped off the check, looking from Dan to Max, obviously uncomfortable. Max broke her gaze from Dan and addressed the woman.

"You good, lady? You need fucking forgiveness or something?" Max said, pulling cash out of her bra and throwing it down. The waitress walked off, not returning the apologetic smile Dan offered as penance.

"I would have paid. Do you need cash?" Dan asked, reaching for his wallet.

"Don't you fucking pity me. I told you, nobody gets to look down on me. I make more money than you, for God's sake," Max said, a little louder than she had intended to.

"Would you calm down?" Dan asked, pulling his collar off and tucking it into his pocket.

Sam laughed. "Yea, take your wedding ring off when you're with your whore, right?" Max asked sarcastically, looking back out the window.

"Jesus Christ," Dan said, making the sign of the cross, which made Max giggle and shake her head.

"We sound like a bad joke. A priest and a stripper walk into a diner..." Max chuckled.

"It would probably have a good punch line at least." Dan laughed and took a drink from his mug.

"I'm pregnant."

Dan thought for a minute.

"I don't get it. Did you leave part of it out?"

Max stared at him. "I'm pregnant. That's not the punch line, Dan. I'm fucking pregnant!" she said, her face turned from witty to terrified. Dan stopped chewing and then continued in slow, long chews until finally swallowing hard.

"What?" It was a simple question, and yet it had so many layers.

"I'm pregnant," Max said, letting the statement hang.

"How?" Dan asked, trying to breathe normally so he wouldn't pass out.

"Well...when a boy and a girl love each other very much..." Max was trying to lighten the situation.

"You know what I mean," Dan said, cutting her off.

"I don't, actually. This is what happens when people have sex." Max said this like it should be obvious.

"We used protection, Max."

"Ya well, not every time we didn't."

"I pulled out."

Max finally laughed. She laughed so hard it made Dan uncomfortable.

"Is that what you teach next to abstinence?" Max asked, gasping between laughs.

"You're sure? I mean, how late are you?"

"Went to the doctor yesterday."

"You're sure it's mine?" He regretted it the moment he said it. His face stung as the sound of her hand slapping his cheek echoed in his head.

"I'm sorry," Dan said, rubbing his cheek.

"Damn right you are," Max said, looking back out the window.

"What are we going to do?" Dan asked, wondering if he should reach for her hands.

"Oh, there is a 'we' now? We're a couple now? Or even a family, huh?"

Dan retreated back against the booth corner. Nothing he said was right, and he didn't think anything he was going to say soon would be right either.

"What do you want me to do?" Max asked, staring hard at Dan.

"It's not up to me."

"Bullshit. What do you want me to do?" It was a simple question, but an impossible one.

"I...Max...this can't." Dan tiptoed around the words.

Max was shaking her head and looked out the window again.

"Don't even worry about it alright?" Max said, getting up out of the booth, ignoring Dan, who was trying to offer a hand to help her out.

"Don't fucking touch me! You think I'm all fragile now just because I'm pregnant?"

Dan shushed her and looked around the room.

"You did not just fucking shush me!" Max said, looking at Dan in astonishment.

"Please, just..." Dan threw his hands up at a loss. Max walked out of the diner and didn't look back to notice Dan did not follow her.

↓ ↓ ↓ ↓ ↓ ↓

Sleep is a funny thing for a priest. It either comes easy or not at all. Tonight, he would be getting none. He replayed the conversation in his head. With each new run, he would give different answers, trying to see the path his life could have taken. He wondered if it was a boy or a girl. Maybe it was both. Twins ran in his family, after all. Twins sounded exhausting but the thought of playing with his children while Max cooked dinner didn't seem as scary as he had first thought.

THE MORNINGSTAR CONFESSION 143

He was shaken from his thoughts by the crucifix staring down at him from his dorm room wall. No, that couldn't happen. He would be gambling with someone else's money. His soul wasn't the only one on the line here. He was responsible for his mother's soul, and that was the bed he had made. He did wonder, though, if his mother would want him to pursue a life with Max. After all, don't all parents want their children to succeed and be happy even at their own peril? His head was swimming. Communion wine had a low alcohol content. It was tough to get drunk off of it. It was tough, not impossible, and Dan had consumed enough to be properly fucked up. The crucifix shifted with the blurs of his vision. The long hair looked more feminine, long strands covered Christ's face. The head swayed, almost as if it were cracking its strained neck. Dan took a long, slow swig of the wine, looking over at the statue with a cautioned curiosity.

"Dannnniiieelll," the crucifix wheezed.

"Nope, definitely not drunk enough for that," Dan said, chugging the remainder of that particular bottle.

"Dannniiieeelll, how is my boyyyyy?" the crucifix asked.

"Are you supposed to sound so creepy? I feel like my drunken talking crucifix mom should sound more appealing, but please carry on."

The crucifix relaxed, its arms falling from the boards and resting on its knees in a crouch.

"It's in your head, my boy. Why do you always go to the dark places?"

Dan chuckled. He was really about to talk to a crucifix. He was hallucinating his dead mother on a crucifix. *Wow.*

"Sometimes the dark stuff is all that makes sense, mom. Sometimes I feel like it's all I deserve."

"You help people, you've helped me."

Dan took another long swig of wine.

"I don't feel very helpful right now, mom. I don't know what to do."

The tiny figure nodded, placing its head on its hands in a thinking pose. "You're worried about me, and what happens if you leave? About breaking the promise you made?"

Dan looked over at her with a frown.

"I understand that you're my conscience or whatever, but could we not lay it on so thick?" Dan pleaded, dropping another bottle of wine.

"You're in control here, son. I'll do what you tell me."

"That's not very helpful then, is it, mom?"

"Tell me what changed?"

Dan thought for a moment until his eyes watered, tears rolling down his face. "I didn't plan on being happy, mom," Dan finally admitted.

Dan started to weep. He covered his eyes, hoping that somehow that would shield his shame as well as his tears. His mother was standing over him now, rubbing his forehead and wiping away the tears. He cried harder with each one she wiped away. Her fingers were the softest, warmest thing he had ever felt. In Dan's head, he was at peace and, at least for tonight, he could pretend that his mother was there to take care of him and not the other way around.

↓ ↓ ↓ ↓ ↓ ↓

"Off communion wine? For someone who knocks up strippers, Dan, you really cheaped out on the booze," the voice mocked.

"Ask already," Dan said, defeated.

"What happened to the baby, Dan? Did you marry Max and live happily ever after?"

Dan didn't even get mad at the mocking tone. He had accepted what had happened between him and Max a long time ago. "I woke up the next morning and washed my face. I looked like someone had hit me with a vineyard. The crucifix had fallen off the wall and shattered, leaving Christ in a million pieces over my floor. I picked up his head and tucked it in my pocket. It felt wrong to leave him or throw him away, ya know?"

"Sure."

"I walked across campus and into Father Mason's office. It had become somewhat like my own private confessional, but this time, I would truly test him. He always seemed so busy, but no matter what, he made time for me. I think we had a mutual respect for our attitudes towards things. I questioned things, and he liked that. I didn't just take 'God has a plan' at face value when I was younger, and I think he took it as a challenge."

"What's new, Dan? Pretty soon I'll be calling you father," he said with a smile, not looking up at his papers.

"I'm leaving," Dan blurted out.

"Ok, I'll see you when you get over whatever this week's crisis is," Father Mason said, still not paying any attention to Dan.

"I got a stripper pregnant." Dan pushed the words out like a child trying to swallow medicine.

Father Mason stopped writing and sat back in his chair.

"Ok. I'll admit that's a new one even for you," he said, placing his hands behind his back. "This isn't a joke, I presume?" Father Mason stared at Dan in disbelief.

He shook his head no, trying to not look away from Father Mason's gaze.

"Would you like me...to speak with her?"

Dan's face muddled up in confusion. "About what?" Dan asked, genuinely curious.

"The church has avenues available to you. To her and you. We have funds set up for...'situations' such as this."

Dan wasn't any less confused. "I'm not sure I know what you mean."

"Yes, you do. You're not dumb, Dan. You made a mistake, but you're not ignorant."

"When you say avenues?"

Father Mason rocked his chair side to side. "The church has many programs for children. We have housing for single mothers."

"She's not a single mother," Dan interrupted, the words sterner than he expected, which surprised even him.

"Dan, this doesn't have to ruin your life. Like I said, the church has things in place. Things like this are more common than you realize."

Dan didn't know how to feel about that. On one hand, he was being offered a lifeline and after the situation he had found himself in, could he really judge anyone for accepting that help?

"I have a responsibility," Dan stated, trying to end any further discussion.

"Yes. Yes, you do to God and to his faithful. You have a responsibility to teach and guide your congregation as your own children. So while you may think you are stepping up to raise this child, what you are doing is, in fact, abandoning all your other children."

Dan's head started to swim. He had accepted the fact he was responsible for this child. This one child which he had created, but hearing Father Mason lay it out like that, he was lost again. He had woken up knowing exactly what he was going to do, and now he was just as unsure and scared as last night.

"Sit down." Father Mason poured whiskey from a decanter and handed him the glass. Dan emptied it in one gulp, and Father Mason quickly refilled it.

"Have you spoken to her?"

"Not since last night," Dan said, sipping from his glass.

"How long has this been going on?"

Dan just looked up at the man.

"Got it. You said she's a stripper?"

"Yes," Dan sighed. Saying it all out loud made him feel so embarrassed.

"Stripper, not hooker?"

Dan shook his head and took another sip. "No, no, nothing like that."

"You are sure it's yours?"

Dan paused and looked at him with a flash of anger.

"Our campus is close to that strip club, Dan. This isn't the first time something like this has happened," Father Mason said, placing his hands up in defense.

Dan's stomach dropped.

"What are you talking about?" Dan asked, listening closely now.

"You're young, hell all of you are young, and you're about to take a vow of celibacy. A lot of you think I'll get this in one last time. I mean, I don't blame you, but a lot of these girls, Dan, they see you guys as a way out. You're good guys, a lot better than what they are used to, and so they latch themselves onto you guys like beautiful leeches."

Dan felt sick to his stomach. "The girl named Max has she ever..." Dan looked down in shame, not knowing what to think anymore.

"Oh kid, I mean that's not her real name but yea, a couple of times," Father Mason said hesitantly. He slid the decanter towards Dan in a show of support. Dan grabbed the neck of the bottle, tossing the heavy glass cap to the side with a thud and started to chug the contents.

"Whoa, whoa there cowboy, let's take it down juuuust a notch, ok?" Father Mason pleaded, grabbing Dan's hands and grasping the decanter. He walked Dan back over to his dorm room and tucked him into bed.

"I'll speak to her and I'll take care of it, alright? Just rest now." Dan heard as the door to his dorm room shut and then locked.

He woke up about 9:38 that evening. Getting blackout drunk for two days in a row was not something he was particularly proud of and not something he would suggest. He downed the water bottle that had been left next to the bed and finished it with a gasp. He would have to campaign to get Father Mason a Sainthood. He needed to see Max, needed to talk to her and set this straight, regardless of what the outcome would be.

↓ ↓ ↓ ↓ ↓ ↓

The lights from the club flashed through the smoke that surrounded the building. The manhole covers were blowing steam like hell was just below the surface. Dan often imagined the world just like that, as if he could dig twenty feet and reach down into some fiery abyss. It was bullshit, but it gave him comfort in an odd way, almost like if these people had to be punished, at least they weren't that far from home. He smiled, thinking about when he was little and they would walk through the graveyard stepping over the corpses below. He and his brother would imagine a city of the dead below them with restaurants, movie theaters and even a library. In all honesty, death didn't seem so bad when you lived in the city of the dead. Plus, he always thought he would make a cool skeleton.

Reality snapped him out of his nostalgia when the bouncer stopped him at the door.

"Hey Jesse," Dan said, waiting for him to open the door like he always did.

"Dan." That was all Jesse said, not indicating any motion toward the door nor any intent of opening it.

"Max working?" Dan asked, his eyes moving from the door to Jesse.

"Naw," Jesse said, crossing his arms and looking out at the corners of the street. Dan looked over his shoulders. Nobody was around, and there were no people walking from any direction toward the club.

"When's her next shift?" Dan asked cautiously.

"She quit two days ago. Came in here real upset about something. We all tried talking to her, but she wasn't having any of it. We figured it had something to do with you. Tell me I'm wrong?"

Dan shook his head from side to side.

"Can't tell you that, unfortunately."

Jesse nodded somberly and then breathed in, shrugging his shoulders. His whole demeanor had changed with those two movements and a much more intimidating person now stood before Dan.

"So management is pretty pissed and word got to them they lost a big money maker thanks to you."

"Rhonda, huh?" Dan said with a smirk.

"Bitches." Jesse shrugged his giant shoulders, as if that should explain everything. "I can't let you in," he said, placing his hands down below his crotch.

"I have to find out where she is, man. I've got to talk to Rhonda," Dan pleaded.

Jesse was already shaking his head or what his massive neck would allow for shaking.

"Ain't happening. I like you, Dan, we all do, but I got a mouth to feed."

Dan rushed for the door. Jesse was huge, but he wasn't fast.

"Motherfucker! Are you kidding?" was all Dan could hear behind him as he slammed the door as hard as he could and locked it behind him. The club wasn't busy, but the music and light drowned out any yelling that Jesse was doing and the bass from the speakers made all the banging sound just like it was part of the song. The bartender stopped cleaning his glass and placed his hands on his hips, watching Dan check each girl as he walked by them. Rhonda wore a different wig every night and Dan, unfortunately, needed to see the girl's face. He did not have the time to be gentle, so pulling the girls' shoulders to expose their faces added to the line of angry people who pursued Dan to the back of the club. Dan felt himself lift off the ground and was rushed through the kitchen and through the door out into the alley.

The air escaped his lungs as Jesse's boot dug into his stomach, lifting him off the ground.

"Are you really making me beat up a fucking priest, dude!?"

The punch connected with Dan's left cheek. His jaw exploded like a million little fists were punching him all at once.

"My Nana would be so fucking pissed at me right now, Dan!" The owner of the club stopped Jesse and instructed him to hold Dan up for him.

"You don't come around here. You don't bug my girls. You don't bug my customers, you understand?"

Before Dan could answer, the man's fist collided with Dan's nose. It wasn't nearly as hard as Jesse's, but the impact was nauseating. The two men left Dan in the fetal position, surrounded by his own blood and spent cigarettes as he drifted away from consciousness.

↓ ↓ ↓ ↓ ↓ ↓

"We shouldn't be doing this." Nobody could see either of them in the dark car and even if they did, two people in a parked car outside of the strip club were nothing out of the ordinary, but Dan was still sweating bullets.

"You kissed me," Max laughed, unbuttoning the top of Dan's shirt and sliding her hands across his chest. Her hands were cold, but they quickly started feeling warm as they lightly hovered across his pecs every once in a while, tightening up at Max's playful squeeze of his nipple.

"You let me kiss you. That's against the rules." His coy smile trying to mask the heart beating out of his chest. Her hands rose to his neck and then behind his head, cradling it like some sort of mother trying to comfort a newborn. He closed his eyes, focusing on his heart booming. The pulse expanding throughout his entire body calmed with her touch. The blood rushing in his ears slowed to a trickle, and the world seemed to quiet down, just for the two of them at that moment. He opened his eyes to see her smiling at him, drawing his own childish grin to spread across his face. She was pleased with herself and the reaction her touch had on him.

"All of my best experiences have started with a bad idea. I'm a stripper and you're a priest. Can you imagine what an experience this will be?" She kissed him long and slow. Each press of her lips was complimented by another tiny kiss placed right after. It was almost as if she was signing off on every little bit of love she was sharing with him. It made him feel good. Like he was wanted for exactly who he was and not what he could offer. He started returning them with his own "stamped" kisses and he enjoyed finding new and innovative ways to show her how much she mattered to him. She leaned back, gazing into his eyes like nobody ever had before. They were brown, nothing flashy or exciting about them, but they promised things of desire and wonder. They promised they would never judge him for who he was or who he had been. They would never leave him alone in this world, navigating the treachery of life and its promises. They would not belittle him for his beliefs and desires, no matter how absurd or adolescent they seemed. They pledged he would be loved and celebrated. They promised to see him.

His hands were pulling her closer, acting on their own impulses and the desire to feel and explore her. She was so tight against him they felt almost like two souls inhabiting the same body ever encircling one another in a constant pursuit of belonging. Time seemed to stop for the two of them. Dan's embarrassment at the quickness it was over melted away as she held him even tighter, pressing her cheek against his as if to say, *I have you.* The giggles that filled the car were precipitated by more kisses giving way to each of them, enjoying the other's body deep into the morning hours.

Max laid on Dan's chest, falling in and out of the land of dreams. The soft rising and lowering of his chest, like an ocean of relaxation, had her barely able to keep her eyes open. Dan was drawing angels amongst a background of clouds. The stick figured little people were crudely drawn, Max noted, but the wings were actually impressive, with individual feathers drawn with meticulous detail.

"You're really good at that."

Dan looked away from the window and smiled at her.

"It's no Sistine Chapel, but thank you."

She nuzzled against him, pointing at the biggest of the angel figures.

"You think they are up there? Watching out for us?"

He cast a glance over his drawing. The tiny faces of each figure seemed to be judging him, awaiting his answer.

"I hope not otherwise, we just gave them a free show."

They both chuckled as he took her hand inside of his, smothering her arm in a Pepé Le Pew stream of kisses.

"Seriously though, what do you think?" She pointed toward the drawing once more. Dan took in a breath, releasing it slowly.

"I think if they are really up there watching they probably hate it."

Max looked over the stick figures, imagining their little faces scowling as they looked down at everyone in bitter judgment.

"No, I don't like that. Tell me something happier," she said in a playful tone.

"Happier, huh?"

She nodded in excitement.

"You're cute."

She smiled even wider, urging him on.

"There is this guy on top of his house and the whole place is flooded, ok?"

Max nodded, listening.

"The water is filling up the first floor when a truck driver yells up offering help but the man just waves him off saying the Lord will provide. The water is now up to the roof and a rescue boat drives right up to the guy but he just shakes his head, saying the Lord will provide. The water gets up to his neck, and he's getting tired of treading water when a helicopter hovers over him, lowering a ladder. He spits the water out of his now almost submerged mouth and says…"

"The Lord will provide!" Max giggled as Dan nodded.

"The man drowns and when he wakes up in heaven, he finds God and really bores into him. Why didn't you save me? I was faithful until the end! God looks at him and says 'I sent you two boats and a helicopter, you idiot.'"

Max applauded, laughing at the story.

"I think that's how God works. At least, that's what makes the most sense to me."

"So, you *do* think somebody is watching?" she accused.

Dan smirked, wiping the window clean of his steamed masterpiece.

"I hope he's watching, but sometimes I fear he isn't even there."

Max held his cheek, letting him know she was there.

"Do you think your mom's watching you?"

Dan was taken aback. He never really discussed his mother with anyone.

"I'm sorry, we don't have to."

"No, it's ok," Dan interrupted. "That's why I do this, at least, that's why I started doing this. Sometimes I'm scared I'm wasting my life doing this, and she's nowhere or worse—in hell."

"I don't think it's fair. Your life is your own and what you do with it or how you end it should be up to you."

Dan nodded.

"At least that's how I think it is," Max said.

"What if you're wrong though?" That question had haunted Dan ever since his mom had decided to end her life. There were rules that needed to be followed. Whether or not he believed in them, the possibility of his mother burning in hell was a very real possibility.

"I think if I'm wrong, then God is an asshole and I wouldn't want to worship an asshole, anyway." She was smiling, but Dan could tell she meant it. There was pain behind her words and her eyes couldn't hide it, no matter what promises they made.

Dan started to feel sick. A chill filled him and crept through his blood at the realization of where he was and what he had done. *If anyone found out...*

"We shouldn't have done this." He wanted to look away from her. Her face upturned in a variegated canvas of hurt that melted into anger. It hurt him to see her like that. To make her look like that.

"Don't ruin this. I know you're scared or whatever bullshit you need to tell yourself, but don't. Just fucking don't."

He breathed in deeply, bracing himself for the pain and confusion this would cause her.

"I'm going to be a priest and you're a stripper, Max. This whole thing is crazy," he said, hoping she would realize how insane this all was.

"So what? Nobody has to know."

"People would notice."

"No, they wouldn't. Stop."

"They would notice and they would spread it every chance they got."

"Stop."

"Then I would get fired and..."

"Stop it!" They sat for a moment in melancholy until Max pushed the door open and exited into the brisk morning, completely naked.

"Are you kidding!" Dan yelled, not knowing if he should just drive off.

"Fuck you!"

"Max, get in the car!"

"Fuck you!" she called as she walked completely nude back into the alley and through the door to the club. Moments later, Rhonda busted through the front door of the club, meaning all business. She scanned the parking lot until she zoned in on Dan. He turned the key and pulled out, leaving Rhonda and her fury in the rearview mirror.

↓ ↓ ↓ ↓ ↓ ↓

Dan woke up filled with anxiety and pain. His head was playing a full on concert of agony with an encore of nausea. When his vision cleared, he saw Rhonda standing over him, smoking a cigarette.

"Fucking pathetic, you know that?" she said, tossing the cigarette down onto his bruised body.

"Rhonda, wait, please. I need to see her!" Dan pleaded, rising as fast as he could.

"No, you don't and you're not going to. She's already long gone," Rhonda said, closing the door behind her. Dan's foot blocked the old wooden thing from closing.

"Rhonda, I need to talk to her and fix this," Dan begged.

"We already took care of it. She came right over here after your little date and we drove to the clinic and took care of it, so tell your church buddies and whoever else to leave her the fuck alone!"

THE MORNINGSTAR CONFESSION   161

The door slammed on Dan's foot again and he removed it. It wasn't from pain though and more out of necessity, so he didn't fall over from the revelation that he had ruined his relationship and been responsible for killing his unborn child.

The walk back to his dormitory seemed like it took years. Each block, Dan was playing over the life he could have had if he hadn't been such a coward. The first street was their baby being born, holding him or her close and promising to always protect them. The second block was their first steps and receiving a call from an ecstatic Max while he was at work. The third block was his child's first break up and trying to reassure them that this heartache would pass, but they would remember this one for the rest of their lives. It went on and on like this, walking through experiences that he would never get to have, making memories with a family that did not have, and now, because of his selfishness, could never exist. He drifted off to sleep that night, ignoring the loneliness and the cold of his bed, and imagined Max and him—safe, warm and together for one last time. The next morning, he was called into Father Mason's office, almost certain he would be expelled. He tried to make himself look presentable, but he could tell by Mason's expression it didn't work.

"Can you explain why I just had a man in confession crying about beating the shit out of a priest?"

Dan shook his head, and pieces of dried blood flaked off, falling onto Father Mason's desk.

"Is this going to be an issue, Dan?"

He once again shook his head no, this time adding a swipe of his hand cleaning the desk of any DNA evidence he was leaving with each denial.

Father Mason sighed at the sight of Dan and leaned back in his chair.

"If the home is worthy, let your peace rest on it; but if it is not?" Father Mason let it hang in the air. Dan tongued the inside of his cheek and stood for the door.

"Let your peace return to you, and if anyone will not receive you or listen, leave that home and shake the dust off your feet," Dan finished, waving goodbye as he exited the office.

"Close enough." Father Mason nodded in approval.

Chapter 8
The Truth is Not in Us

"So, you abandoned her and here we are, eh, Dan?"

"I didn't leave. I didn't abandon anyone. I went back to have a life with her."

"No, Dan, you went back so you could have a life for you."

Dan was about to tell the voice that wasn't true, but he stopped himself. He didn't have the energy anymore. He was tired of all this.

"Fuck you."

"There he is."

"You don't know me. You don't know how I feel or the guilt I feel every night."

"I do, Dan. Trust me, I know it better than you do," the voice chuckled.

Dan didn't want to talk anymore. He wanted out of this shitty box, this shitty church, and this shitty existence. Dan tried to calm himself. This wasn't him.

"This is what you do, isn't it? It's not always giant things. It's burnt coffee, a missed bill, bringing up losing the fucking love of your life," Dan explained.

"I just point out things that you fuck up, Dan. I don't create them."

"I certainly did fuck up," Dan surrendered.

"Some accountability, finally."

"At least I admit I fucked up as a parent."

"I've never been a parent, Dan."

"That's one thing you and I can agree on," Dan chuckled.

"If you want to say something, I suggest you spit it out before I rip out your entrails."

"You abandoned him. He didn't do what you wanted, so you left and never went back to help."

The voice was silent for a long time. It almost made Dan uncomfortable.

"I went back..."

"I'm sure you were a big help."

"No, I don't think I was," the voice lamented.

"My turn then. Why did you abandon him, let him be tortured?"

"When someone is determined to do something, Dan, there is no persuading them otherwise, even with me in their ear."

Dan was already shaking his head before the voice was finished.

"Absolute bullshit. You can persuade anyone."

"Have you been listening at all? I can't make anyone do anything, especially Him."

"Tell me then. Tell me how you were powerless to help."

The voice hesitated, choosing his words carefully.

"Fine. I'll tell you about the last time I saw him."

"Good." Dan felt like he had won something.

"On the condition that we end this. You forgive me and we be done with this night."

It was Dan's turn to hesitate. He had not really thought about what would happen if he didn't forgive the voice. Would he be stuck here forever? Would he constantly be throwing up and shitting creatures? That last thought made him wince.

"What if I decide you don't deserve forgiveness?" Dan asked cautiously.

"Have you ever done that before?"

"No..." Dan admitted.

"Then I expect the same treatment as anyone else coming into this box."

"And if I don't..." Dan let the question hang in the air.

"Use your imagination, Dan, and think of the worst things imaginable being done to you. And when that's over and you're cowering, pissing yourself in the corner, I can promise you it's not even close to what I will do."

Dan shuddered, his penis retracted inside his stomach like a turtle retreating into its shell.

"Go on then," Dan coughed out.

↓ ↓ ↓ ↓ ↓ ↓

"He has not done anything," Pontius stated, dumbfounded as he addressed the angry crowd gathered beneath his chambers. They murmured amongst themselves about the Nazarene and his blasphemous claims, about how he was said to perform miracles, or that he was the son of Jehovah. One figure among them stood in the back, hiding, his death-like stare boring into the skull of Joshua. Lucifer was not happy about any of this. Something about it made his throat sink into the pit of his stomach. The situation made his feet itch as if he needed to run or get far away. He stood there for a long time contemplating leaving Joshua to deal with whatever this mess was about. Then the Roman brought out another prisoner named Barabbas in chains. Lucifer felt a sense of relief when the Roman offered up a choice for the pardon. It would be Joshua or the murderer.

They were hesitating. They were actually entertaining the choice. Lucifer pulled the hood from his head, revealing a generic-looking man as he moved closer through the crowd.

"Who should be pardoned?" the Roman asked again, this time a little more forceful.

Part of the crowd called out, "Barabbas!"

The so-called Christ!" the rest answered back.

The Morningstar was not surprised easily and yet here he stood; mouth almost agape. Pilot looked at Joshua with a glint of pain in his eyes and then back to the crowd. With a flick of his wrist, Barabbas's chains were unfastened, and the man laughed his way out of the courtyard.

The commotion of the murderer laughing his way through the crowd drew more to gather outside the temple, and Lucifer, more than once, was pushed along with the crowd's general flow of direction. He needed to find Joshua and see what that stupid boy had gotten himself into before this got worse.

The crowd parted with some vomiting and others defecating. Lucifer was in no mood to push his way through these fools, plus he liked the faces the others made as they mocked or turned away in disgust. The crowds were separating along the sides of a street, making themselves comfortable, exchanging pleasantries, and speaking of the things Joshua had been preaching. Lucifer listened in on the group closest to the office where Joshua was about to be led out of.

"He was throwing the tables over shaming the Rabbis and all who allowed it."

"Healed the man's sight, he did."

"King of the Jews."

"Can walk along the water!"

"Not right, not natural."

Lucifer was shaking his head more and more with each new statement and accusation among the crowd.

"Stupid, foolish boy," the Morningstar proclaimed in frustration, steadying his pace toward the door that held Joshua. Suddenly, his whole body felt incredibly heavy and with each strained push, the dirt broke and deepened around him. He had never experienced a power like this before. It made him panic for only a moment before realizing it had to have been Joshua. He was keeping him away. Lucifer retreated a couple of steps and leaned into the wall, staring at the closed door. He felt conflicted. On one hand, he was impressed with Joshua's display of power. On the other hand, he was being kept from helping Joshua and, most troublesome of all, Joshua was the one keeping him from It. The boy wanted this to happen. He was allowing it, and now he was keeping anyone from interfering. He made his way back amongst the chattering apes, contemplating how any of them made it this far into existence.

"They are searching for his followers."

"Won't find them. Nobody is going to get crucified along with him."

The gossip was useful at least but left him very frustrated. Somebody had told them where Joshua had been. He found the nearest legionnaire and peered into his eyes. "Tell me everything you know about the prisoner, Joshua."

The Roman looked like he was in immense discomfort, but the words were dislodging their way out.

"He...he claims to be the Jew's God. The people...want him...gone...dead. He does not deny it."

Lucifer rubbed his forehead in frustration.

Stupid boy, he thought to himself as he shook away his frustrations.

"Who told you where he and his followers were staying?"

"One of his men. I don't know his name."

He began toward the next soldier as this one was released from his will. The possessed man was drawing attention as he fell to his knees, coughing and trying to catch his breath. Lucifer snapped his fingers in front of the new soldier who was making his way to help, stopping him mid-stride.

"The follower of the prisoner. Who betrayed him? I want his name and where he is currently." The words coursed with venom.

"He was paid and then he retreated to the fields near the trees. He is called Judas." The soldier went back to his task at hand, checking on the other Roman. Lucifer wrapped his cloak tightly and strode out toward the fields to find the man who had betrayed Joshua. He wanted a word with this one.

↓ ↓ ↓ ↓ ↓ ↓

The man was sitting in the shade of a large tree, flipping a coin in the air without a care in the world and letting it land amongst the pile that lay at his feet. When he was done with one, he would pick another and continue the same sequence. The rhythm of the coin was solid and focused until Judas was startled by a hand that had seemed to appear from nowhere and grasped the coin mid-spin. Judas' eyes went to the hand, then to the chest, and finally rested on the face of the man wrapped in robes.

"How much is here?" he asked, placing his hands behind his back as he paced back and forth before the pile of coins.

"I...um... I don't..." Judas said, but to his astonishment, the coin that was stolen was now hovering in front of him. It came inches from Judas' nose, spinning with a velocity that would rip the skin clean off of it.

"I asked how much!" With a snap of his right hand, the coin flipped into the air and bounced off of Judas' head. The coin ripped hair and flesh and then proceeded on its path, landing once again to hover inches from Judas's nose.

"How are you doing this?" he asked as he comforted his wound with one hand, trying to shield himself with the other.

The coin came again, this time bouncing off of his skull with a thud, taking more skin and hair with it like a payment of flesh.

"I SAID HOW MUCH WAS HIS LIFE WORTH TO YOU?" Lucifer bellowed, sending coin after coin against Judas' cries like some deadly game of TiddlyWinks.

"Thirty! It's thirty pieces! Take it! Just please stop," he begged, cowering in fear of what he couldn't explain.

Lucifer stopped pacing, grasping one of the coins and pressing it between his thumb and forefinger.

"Thirty pieces," he laughed, looking back into town and the crowd that had gathered for Joshua's execution. He walked toward Judas. His presence emanated an energy that could only be described as hostile, causing the man to cower and fall to his knees in dread.

"You heard him speak?"

Judas nodded, trying to wipe the snot and tears forming on his quivering lips.

"You followed him until now?"

He kept nodding, this time sobbing into his hands. Lucifer shook his head in disbelief, stood and placed his hand tight around the back of Judas' neck, forcing him to look him in the eyes. No words were uttered, but everything that ever had or would be conversed filled Judas's mind in a cloud of clairvoyance. He saw Joshua and what was about to happen. He saw the wars and the hate that would fill this land and all others once Joshua's side was pierced with a dirty spear. He tore at his eyes, only stopped from reaching his intended targets because Lucifer forbid it somehow. He wanted desperately to not be able to see what he had done, to not see what the world would turn into because of his betrayal, but it was made sure he saw all of it.

"He may look the other way. He might teach that you should forgive, do better, be better," Lucifer hissed through gritted teeth.

Judas stopped sobbing long enough to look at the man, whose features no longer resembled anything human. What stood before him made his bowels empty in the field and piss run down his leg. It made his stomach churn and spew streams of vomit. It stung his eyes, emptying tears until it felt as though he would run dry. He felt like fleeing and hiding, but his body betrayed him. His nerves and limbs were not in unison. He collapsed to his knees and curled up like he had in the womb, trying to comfort himself in a pool made of his own filth instead of his mother's stomach.

"Maybe hell will forgive me for what I'm going to do to you," the Morningstar mused as he made his way toward the village, ignoring the anguished and horrified wails behind him.

Judas lay still praying for the terror to leave, for the fear to empty out of him, and for him to not feel so cosmically alone. His prayers went unanswered.

↓ ↓ ↓ ↓ ↓ ↓

Lucifer moved faster with each scream he heard. They were Joshua's. He felt it in his bones. It made his stomach feel tight and sour. It was a sensation that he had not experienced before and he did not enjoy it. The feeling of nausea made his steps faster, hoping to shake off the feeling of the sour in his guts. The sight before him did nothing to steady him. Joshua was tied to a post. His back resembled torn curtains marinated in blood. The Roman who was whipping him cocked back for another blow but held his arm high and ready to strike. Lucifer made sure that the weight of that blow would be too heavy for any human and suddenly the whip cracked and returned with bits of Joshua's flesh parading the Roman like confetti.

"You want this to happen," Lucifer said to himself.

It was a question as much as a statement. Joshua was keeping him out, keeping him from protecting him, even from torture. Lucifer dared himself to step closer, fighting back the urge to make these people disappear, to make them all go away so he could talk some sense into the boy. The whip cracked, causing cheers from some and cries from others. Lucifer watched the expressions amongst the crowd. Some smiled, some laughed, while others wailed and screamed for mercy.

"Serves him right."

Lucifer turned slowly to face the man who said it. The man's expression showed he immediately regretted saying it.

"I just meant saying he's the son of God and all," the man said back peddling.

Lucifer smiled, causing the man even more discomfort. The man wiped at the beads of sweat suddenly building on his forehead.

"It's blasphemy," the man was trying anything to win Lucifer to his side. Lucifer smiled even wider.

"Blasphemy is indeed worthy of death, torture even."

The man smiled and nodded, finally relaxing at Lucifer's agreement.

"Do you go to temple?"

The man was about to answer, but noticed Lucifer's smile had grown unnaturally large somehow.

"I...I do," the man answered cautiously, turning only briefly to look at Joshua and then back at the grotesque smile which seemed to be getting bigger.

"I have not been in...well a long time," Lucifer said, cocking his head to the side and grinning even wider.

"Are you Roman?" the man asked, clearly uncomfortable with the unnatural grin.

"I am a great many things to a great many people. Some would even say a blasphemer."

Lucifer's grin split, stretching the flesh in half like long strings of cheese. The man screamed and turned to look for help from the crowd, but they were gone. It was just him and the man with the awful grin, laughing and walking towards him. He ran as fast as he could, looking back to see blood pouring from the mouth as the man's smile widened beyond its physical limits. Eventually the lips curled back, exposing flesh and bone beneath.

"Dear Lord, help me!" he cried, falling over his own feet. Then the man was next to him and suddenly, he was face to face with an exposed skull that laughed at him.

"He can't help you. He's a little distracted at the moment!" the skull yelled inches from his face, causing him to shut his eyes so tight his cheeks ached.

"What the fuck are you yelling about?"

The sound assaulted him from all sides, causing his head to ache and nausea to set in his stomach. The crowd was back suddenly, with no sign of the horrible man anywhere.

"I said what the fuck is wrong with you, Jew?" The Roman soldier asked, grabbing the man by the robe and pulling him down next to Joshua.

"What's your name?" the Roman yelled, kicking the man over so his face was mere inches from Joshua's.

"Simon," he uttered, trying to avoid Joshua's gaze. The Roman ordered him to help carry the cross, which Joshua could no longer drag. Simon began to protest and retreat back into the crowd when the skeleton with the flayed face waved to him in the crowd. He turned quickly and shielded his eyes from the horrible sight, only to be met with Joshua's battered and bruised face.

"He will not harm you," Joshua said through painful breaths.

Simon cautiously uncovered his eyes and looked into Joshua's.

"You can see him?" Simon asked, thankful that he was not going mad.

"We all can see him. We all ignore him until it's too late," Joshua lamented.

"Carry it!" The Roman commanded once again, snapping Simon's attention away.

He looked out among the crowd but couldn't find the skeleton. He breathed a sigh of relief until the Roman kicked him hard in the shoulder, finally pressing him to lift the heavy wooden cross.

↓ ↓ ↓ ↓ ↓ ↓

Veronica was regretting ever coming into the square. She had heard of the man and his claims, but like everyone else, she was curious if he would perform some sort of miracle and escape. It was an exciting thought, but from the cries and roar of the crowd, it seemed that he was no messiah and out of useful magic tricks. The crowd was growing more restless with each passing moment. Confliction divided the crowd. Half for even more barbarism to be inflicted on the man, the other wanting it to cease immediately. Veronica couldn't say which one of the two was justified, but the entire ordeal seemed horrific.

She had thought to just retreat into her home and to drown the sound of the poor man's bellowing, but that task seemed impossible. His anguish echoed inside her skull like someone was delivering each scream personally and only finding comfort the closer she got to the man. She needed the pain to stop. Something was pulling her closer, making her crave seeing the poor bastard who was being tortured.

A man appeared before her, his arm extended, producing a shroud.

"Go before him and clean him. Make him presentable as much as you can."

Veronica started to protest, not wanting to get involved, when he interrupted her.

"Clean him as best you can, comfort him," the man said, tossing the shroud over.

"Please, make the pain go away. I can't stand it anymore."

"Don't worry, he will, despite what you all have done to him."

Lucifer called over his shoulder.

↓ ↓ ↓ ↓ ↓ ↓

"He's very young," Kazia said, pinching Rose's cheek as hard as she could until a stream of tears started flowing down her soft cheeks.

"He's very cute. I mean, not now, obviously," Rose said, gathering a laugh from the other girls.

"Girls," Alexandra scolded, pointing over to the condemned man's mother. She sat almost catatonic despite the shaking. Her eyes were puffy and looked as though each tear she shed took a year of her life with it. Kazia felt bad for her, but she was paid to cry. With each wail, she hoped that it brought relief and comfort to the loved ones of the men she had witnessed being nailed to the old wood.

"Tell me something."

The words startled her as she turned toward the voice, who appeared out of nowhere.

"How can you tell when you're actually crestfallen anymore?"

Kazia felt uneasy around him but stepped closer to answer him still.

"What do you mean, sir?" she asked politely since she couldn't tell the man's status from his robes. It was better to be safe than sorry.

"Do you know why you *things* cry?"

The man was talking more to himself than to her, but she listened anyway. "You are greedy. You learned ever since you slithered out of your mother's cunt that if you cry, someone will come running and place a tit into your mouth."

Kazia was taken aback at the boldness of the man. Lucifer wasn't usually so coarse, but he was growing more agitated.

"How dare you!" Kazia called, drawing the attention of the other women. Alexandra and Rose moved up beside her, letting her know they were there.

"We provide a service and we help people grieve," Rose said confidently.

"You're leeches. Nothing more. You whore your emotions and make a mockery of suffering," the man proclaimed. The women started to protest, but he placed his hand up and uttered only a single word.

"Grieve."

The women stopped talking. Rose's eyes widened and her stomach leapt into her throat. Kristine felt a cold that burrowed into her bones while Alexandra's entire body felt old and sluggish, and then the pain came. It overtook the three women's hearts so fast that if they had knives, they would have gladly carved them out in hope of relief. The women felt the pain of every mother losing a child, of family members, and murdered sons and daughters. Every lost elder in the village. They felt each loss like it was their own and they fell to their knees and cried out to the Lord to stop the pain.

Lucifer walked over to the woman staring down the path at her son, making his painful climb toward her. He placed his hand on her shoulder and instantly pulled it back. Her touch burned like no fire he had ever experienced, and he had experienced them all. The woman turned briefly, enough to acknowledge who he was and then turned back to her son, not caring at all who he was or why he was there.

Lucifer did not like being ignored and usually he would make the woman pay, but he had more pressing matters to attend to. At least that's what he told himself as he walked toward the hill where the others waited.

↓ ↓ ↓ ↓ ↓ ↓

"Get these two strung up already," Longinus said, spitting onto the dirt. He hated this duty. He would much rather be marching in some foreign land or even on guard detail, but his eyes held him back from anything truly exciting and so it seemed crucifixions would be the highlight of his military career. Today was slightly more exciting. The Jews had been in an uproar about some carpenter claiming to be the messiah and, unfortunately for the carpenter, it didn't look like he had any powers to get himself out of being nailed to the cross.

"He'll be here soon. I want both of these ones ready to go!"

The two men looked like complete opposites. One stared ahead at the monstrosity of carved wood, contemplating how he had ended up here and who was to blame for his misfortune. The other was looking everywhere, desperately seeking a way out of this predicament and for whom he needed to speak to for release.

"There has been a mistake! Please let me go! I have money! You can have it all," the nervous one begged. Longinus usually enjoyed the begging. He didn't know if the man was telling the truth. That wasn't his job nor his responsibility, and he didn't like questioning whether what he was doing was just. So he had learned to condemn them all. If a man had been found guilty before arriving at his hill, then that was the end of it. It made his sleep easier and the entertainment level a lot higher.

Who wouldn't want to hear the guilty fear for their lives? Show true terror for what they had done. It was a cosmic justice, one that Jupiter demanded of all men. Jews were an interesting lot. They worshiped a God that seemed weak. No wonder they kept getting enslaved.

"They are actually favored by him."

Longinus was startled by the man who had appeared beside him out of nowhere, stepping back and placing his hand on his gladius.

"Makes me flinch at how he must treat the rest of you," the man said, turning his stare from the two men being laid upon the crosses and directly at him.

"They are lucky we don't grow tired of them in chains and just eradicate them," Longinus said, swiping his hand across the sky for emphasis.

"Lucky, you are indeed," the man said, looking down the hill toward Joshua. He was speaking to his mother and reassuring her that this was how it had to be.

"I don't understand, and not a lot puzzles me, Roman."

Longinus's confusion spread across his face.

"Why is he letting you do this to him? Why does he constantly let you do this to him?" Lucifer paused to contemplate.

"It's love." The answer came from behind him, where a woman was making her way up from the crowd below. Lucifer wasn't impressed easily, but the girl had a beauty to her and a confidence that made him ignore the idiot Roman and gravitate to her. He smelled something on her, like a lingering aroma of burnt wood. It was embedded into her soul.

"I've been inside you."

The words struck Mary Magdalene, but only briefly. She had learned to put aside her shame for her past life.

"I no longer lead that life," Mary said, trying to push past the man.

"You've had my children inside of you," Lucifer said, grabbing her arm and sniffing deeper.

Mary began to protest but realized with horror the man was not speaking about sex.

"Joshua cleared them out of you...*sniff*...and then fell in love."

Mary's fear dissipated as the last statement set in.

"That's... He loves us all," Mary said, pulling her arm free of the man.

"Why is he doing this?" Lucifer asked, pointing down at Joshua.

"I don't know why," Mary said, focusing on Joshua

"But I know that I have faith in him and that he loves us."

Lucifer rolled his eyes and rubbed his forehead.

"I can't tell if you're monkeys or sheep anymore. Every decade I don't think you can get worse, but you do. WHY!?"

Lucifer's voice shook the hill, causing all around him to grasp onto what they could—fearing it was an earthquake. All except Mary, who stood and placed her hand on Lucifer's face. He didn't pull away to both of their amazement.

"We are not going to understand everything. We are not meant to. What we can do is accept that he has a plan and he is following it through."

Lucifer looked toward Joshua. His flesh was hanging off him in strips, his head leaked with sweat and gore, and he was swollen from the suffering he had endured. He slapped the woman's hand away.

"If I want a whore to touch me, I'll pay her," he said, disappearing into the crowd that had gathered at the hill.

↓ ↓ ↓ ↓ ↓ ↓

Longinus took a handful of Joshua's hair, leading him to the three soldiers who were kicking and taunting the other condemned men. Longinus was pulling hard, like trying to make a bitch heel, but the Jew was not fighting him. He couldn't tell if the man was ignoring the pain, or he was simply too exhausted to put up any kind of resistance. He finally gave up trying to get a reaction from the man and tossed him down to the dirt, wiping his hand on the tattered robe of the gore and sweat that had produced a thick film on his hand. The soldiers stripped him of his clothes and laid him down across the thick beam of wood.

Lucifer looked on, waiting for Joshua to end this charade. He had surely proven his point by now, whatever it was. Maybe it was to show that he could take whatever could be thrown at him. His father was full of himself and a show of might—be it a strange way to display it—was very much up his father's alley. He had wondered if the wall that was between his connection to Joshua was his father's doing, but deep down he knew that it was Joshua himself who was keeping him out and not allowing his assistance.

He crept closer, fighting the pain that spread through his body like a slow burning ice. Each step felt heavier and more painful than the last. The Romans lined up Joshua's hands and then brought a wooden mallet down on the iron spikes, spraying a fountain of crimson up toward the heavens. Joshua's cries urged Lucifer on through the pain, finally making his way to the foot of the cross just as Joshua was raised up.

"Talk to me, damn you!" Lucifer cried through the wind and commotion of the crowd.

Joshua stared down; his one non-swollen eye transfixed on Lucifer as he said nothing still.

The Romans held up Joshua's robes, feeling the quality of the fabric.

"We'll draw lots for it!" the Romans laughed, gathering around the pile.

"Fine then," Lucifer said, maintaining his staring match with Joshua while also holding his hand out toward the soldiers. The Romans' eyes flickered, filling with a milky liquid. The smallest among them pushed the largest, causing him to stumble off the cliff, falling to the ground below with a sickening thud. The crowd backed away from the three remaining soldiers, who were snarling and biting at the air towards each other.

One of the Romans was holding Joshua's garments tight to his chest and growling at any who looked his way. Lucifer raised his other hand toward a group of men taunting the man on the cross to Joshua's right. Two immediately grabbed their friend, kicking and punching him until he fell to the ground. The crowd looked on in horror as the men took turns mauling their comrade, an uncontrollable rage emanated from their eyes as they continued to manhandle him. His face was so swollen it hid any clue of emotion, but if they could gaze upon it beneath the blood and the contusions, they would witness a look of utter shock and betrayal.

"These people, these creatures, don't deserve you! They will continue to be a stain on this planet and all who have the misfortune of occupying it with them. You come here to save them and what do they do? LOOK WHAT THEY DID TO YOU! LOOK WHAT YOU DID TO HIM!"

Spittle erupted from the Morningstar's mouth with each word as if it was trying to escape the very rage it was conjured from. The glower that Lucifer spread over the crowd made his eyes gleam, looking hot to the touch, two smoldering coals of hatred and sadness passing judgment at the people gathered at Golgotha.

The crowd erupted into a kaleidoscope of mixed emotions. Some showed their rage, plunging their thumbs into the eyes of the person next to them. Others laughed and threw insults and curses. The mourners continued their anguish, feeling the pain and anger pulsating like bells ringing inside them. Lucifer's sadness swirling into the only thing that made the unbearable feeling of seeing Joshua like this evanesce—hate. Joshua finally was speaking, crying up to their father. Lucifer couldn't hear him, however. The pounding of the blood in his ears reverberated throughout his entire skull like an alarm ringing only for him. It took him a moment to realize that Joshua was calling, not up above, but down to him.

"Father," Joshua said once again, looking at Lucifer with his one perfect eye. A heaviness lingered within it, promising everything would be all right, yet threatening that nothing would ever be the same. The pounding dissipated, words sneaking their way into his head while enveloping his heart with shock. The feeling was unlike anything he had ever experienced. He had witnessed creation, he had been in God's presence, and these things paled in comparison to the feeling Joshua's gaze had over him now. He was being seen for the first time. The feeling did not last long as the realization of what was happening sobered Lucifer, and he turned away in denial. Joshua was not going to be saved by him or anyone else, including their father. Lucifer laid his hand atop the spike that pierced Joshua's feet and compelled himself to return the gaze. He cried above the wails and curses of the crowd, never looking away.

"Father...forgive them...for they know not what they do."

Joshua wasn't stopping him. He was not forcing him to stop tormenting these people. He was simply asking. Lucifer breathed in deep trying to decide his next course of action. He brought his hands down hard, snapping the Romans and Jews out of the trance they had been in. He turned away from Joshua and looked out at the horrified crowd as they soothed themselves and helped the injured around them. His stomach was in knots. Tidal waves of nausea churned in his stomach as his anger grew, slowly spreading through his entire body. His bones felt as if they were made of ice. The coldness enveloped him. Not only external, but inside him as well, sprinkling with it a sense of dread and hopelessness. It was loneliness. It was a horrible feeling, almost like someone had opened his stomach and put all the negativity of creation inside of it.

He had felt close to this only one time in his entire existence and thinking of it only added to the weight of the grief inside him. When his father had turned away from him in heaven that day, banishing him from ever feeling his paternal love or gratification, Lucifer thought nothing would ever smell sweet to his nose. He would never savor the flavors of the elements and the feast that grew upon the earth on his tongue. He would never look out at creation and smile at the simplicity of life and all its perfect chaos. He had felt alone, discarded, abandoned, and now these same unworthy *things* were taking Joshua away from him. Lucifer shook his head, turning his back on the last thing he ever cared about, and uttered only a single word as he disappeared, a single tear smoldering down his defeated cheek.

"No."

Chapter 9
The Greatest Trick

Dan's head was spinning. This was too much, too quick. He had so many questions, and he didn't know where to begin. He foolishly thought he would have some answers when this whole thing was said and done. Instead, he had more questions than when they had started this "confession".

"That's why you hate us? Because we crucified him?" Dan asked, astonished.

"You took the one thing that could have saved your miserable little race and drove nails into it. He came to you offering a way to live and be happy and instead you mocked him and tortured him. None of you deserve him," the voice said, dripping with hatred.

"We all deserve him. I think you missed what he was doing for us. He sacrificed himself so that we could be forgiven."

"And I'm saying you don't deserve to be forgiven. You don't deserve to walk this fucking planet after what you did to him."

"It's easy to be angry. It's easy to wallow in our own sadness thinking that God has left us. It's much harder to remain faithful to something you feel constantly hurts you, but that is what love is. To remain faithful even when other easier avenues are available."

"Don't talk to me about faith and love, Dan. I've seen how you treat those you claim to love."

Dan was about to lash out. To curse this fucking voice and its accusations. But then he realized the voice was right. He thought about Max and the baby they could have had, and then he thought of the moment he knew he was in love.

"Do you know what comfort food is?" Dan asked, almost giggling.

"Is that a serious question, Dan?"

"I was just thinking how you hate us and how no matter what I do, you somehow tear it down and give me a feeling of sadness." Dan said, finally giving into the laughter.

"I don't think you know what comfort food is," the voice said, confused about where Dan was going with this.

↓ ↓ ↓ ↓ ↓ ↓

It worked every time, Dan thought to himself. Every time he looked around at all the people sitting around eating. More people would be lined up at the door, engaging in conversations and speaking about that morning's sermon. The students had been assigned with getting the most number of people they could to attend on Sunday morning. Others in his class had tried everything from flyers to canvassing the neighborhood. One even showed some old films he had found, offering free popcorn. Dan had known the secret to getting people all along, though.

"Pancakes," Dan said, handing stack after stack to the busy line. Father Mason had congratulated him on the "A" already and reminded Dan every time he came back for another plate.

"So, do you make all these yourself, or do you buy the frozen cheap ones from Walmart?"

Dan looked up to see Max smirking, holding out her plate.

"I'll have you know these are my own recipe, but I make better waffles. It's nice to see you didn't burst into flames as you walked in," Dan said, smiling and placing a big stack onto Max's plate.

"I'm never going to be able to eat all those," Max said, eyeing the leaning stack.

"Care to help a lady out?" Max said, eyeing the empty table that had just become available.

Dan knew he shouldn't, but he was surrounded by people and in the church. What could really happen?

"I would be happy to," Dan said, motioning for one of the other students to take his place as he and Max settled at the table.

"So not working today?" Dan smiled at her. Max took a bite of the pancakes and smirked.

"It's Sunday, can't work on the Sabbath right?"

"That's Judaism," Dan laughed, stabbing a chunk out of the stack and scarfing it down.

"What's the difference? You all believe in God, don't ya?" Max said innocently.

"More or less," Dan said, waggling his head between bites.

"No, nobody comes to the club this early. Especially on Sundays."

Dan figured as much. He was sure a lot of the men who frequented the club probably attended church just as regularly.

"Do you recognize anyone?" Dan asked, leaning in so nobody would hear.

Max laughed, wiping syrup off her lips with a napkin.

"Besides you? Sure."

Dan smirked, but looked around to see if anyone had heard.

"Do tell," Dan said, eyeing the four corners of the room, and then looked back at Max.

She sat back and crossed her arms, shaking her head.

"Na, na, na, na, na, sir. I keep secrets just as well as you do...even better, maybe."

Dan sat back, smiling at his defeat.

"Well, it's good to know you can keep secrets, I guess." He let the invitation hang in the air. Max smiled, carving into another stack.

"These are good. Really good, actually."

Dan smiled, holding up his fork in honor. Syrup dripped off the brown, buttery mush.

"My mom taught me how to make them. It was one of the last things we did together. They make me feel close to her," Dan said, taking a quick bite and smiling, hoping he didn't ruin the flirting. To his surprise, Max reached out and placed her hand on top of his.

"That's really nice. Is it true?"

Dan was shocked again at the question.

"Why would I lie about it?"

"People lie. People lie to me especially. It's nice when I hear something genuine," Max said, acting like it wasn't that weird of a question.

"Before my mom went upstairs and killed herself, she taught me to make pancakes," Dan said, standing up and pushing his seat in.

"Enjoy your pancakes." He had turned to leave when Max grabbed his arm.

"Hey, I'm sorry, ok. I can't separate the good ones from the bad ones."

Dan looked into her eyes and instantly felt calmer.

"You're saying I'm a good one?" He grinned, breaking the tension.

"Man, if you're not, then that is some false advertising." Max giggled, pulling him back down to finish the plate.

"So why did you come?" He was back to flirting.

"I wanted to talk to you without my tits out, and I wanted to get to know you."

"I appreciate that, but I'm not exactly single."

"You have a girlfriend?" Max laughed a little too harshly.

"Hey now. I have plenty of dating prospects, thank you."

They both giggled as Max gave him a "sure, sure" nod. Dan looked around the room. It was obvious they were flirting, but nobody seemed to notice.

"I can't have a relationship." He said it with a hint of sadness to it. Max nodded, finishing the last bite of the gooey mess.

"Well, at least we'll always have the pancakes, right?" Max smiled at Dan as he offered his hand out to her. She grabbed it, pulling him into a hug. She felt warm, smelled delicious, and most of all, made him feel safe. Max went to pull away, but Dan held her closer, lingering on the moment they were sharing for as long as he could. Max finally pulled an arm's length away and smiled at him, keeping contact with his hand and his eyes until she needed to let go to see where she was going.

✦ ✦ ✦ ✦ ✦ ✦

"I fucked everything up with her. Maybe I don't deserve forgiveness from her or Christ, but she's one of the good ones. People like her are why Jesus or Joshua, whatever you want to call him, did what he did. Because people like her deserve a clean start when they ask for it. You want me to forgive you, for turning away, for rebelling, for hating us? I'm not really sure, but I can't do that. I won't do that because even if what has been said about you isn't true, you're not sorry."

Lucifer ripped the partition out with the swipe of one sharp claw. His gaze met Dan's as the fear gave way to recognition across his face.

"Do you want to know where that little bitch is, Dan? Where that mouth breathing little pup of yours is?"

Dan's heart skipped a beat at the revelation.

"No, she had an abortion. Rhonda said..."

"She lied to you. Made you think it was true so you would leave Max alone, but your child is very much alive. You can be with them again. All you have to do is forgive me."

Dan fell back against his seat, taking in the information. He thought back to Rhonda and how he should have pushed more. He should have tried harder; he should have been better.

"How do I know you're not lying?" Dan asked, like he was already defeated.

"Look into my eyes and tell me I'm lying."

Dan looked back into the Devil's bright green eyes. His hair was tied back into a neat ponytail, and he wore a white suit with a black vest. Around his neck hung a braided leather cord with the tiny skull of some animal at the bottom. He looked like any other attractive man that would pass through this old wooden building, but there was something about him. Dan knew he was telling the truth.

"No." Dan started to cry, fighting back the urge to change his mind. Suddenly, he heard crashing all around the outside of the confessional.

"I will tear this piece of shit you call a church into pebbles and bring it down right on top of your ugly meat suit. Do you fucking hear me?"

Dan thought back to his teachings, back to his training. There had to be something.

"I cast you out, unclean spirit, along with every Satanic..." Dan was interrupted by Lucifer's roaring laughter.

"Are you fucking kidding me, Dan? Are you trying an exorcism?" The Devil was laughing through the hole, his mouth stretching and taking up the entire opening. His mouth cackled, closing only to catch a breath for another long bout of feverish laughter, each time opening with a new set of rotten or sharpened teeth like a viewfinder straight from hell.

"I'm going to kill you and then I'm going to find that bitch and her pup and make her feel pain on a cosmic level. Ways that you can't even imagine, Dan. I will play her nerve endings like a violin and create a symphony out of their screams. And when their hearts finally give out, I'm going to drag their souls down to the deepest, darkest pit I have until their souls cry out, offering anything and everything they have for me to stop. Then I'll bring your mother to join them."

Dan cried out, punching the wall next to the mouth, daring not to stick his hand in that open maw.

"When they cry up to my father for help and beg for forgiveness for whatever they did to come into my company. Why me, oh Lord? What terrible sin did I commit to offend you? I'll simply tell them they did nothing, and they are there because you were too much of a coward."

Dan didn't see a way out of this. He couldn't tear the images of Max having every carnal act forced upon her by God knows what. His child being roasted on a spit while demons cut off slivers of his fatty flesh, chewing it in long hard smacks. And finally, of his mother, back on the crucifix like that drunken fever dream, only this time having nails driven into any visible piece of skin like a human pincushion. Dan shifted his feet, kicking his right shoe off, spilling the urine that had almost filled the entire shoe.

He started to pray. He prayed that whatever happened to him that Max and his child would be ok and that hopefully his life of servitude bought his mom a way to heaven or at least out of hell. The old wood of the confessional groaned, splitting a crack just wide enough for Dan to see the chaos reigning inside his church. The pews were being thrown against the walls, shattering into a thousand little splinters. The bibles were floating midair; the pages turning so fast that they erupted into floating balls of fire. Amidst all the chaos, the giant crucifix was left untouched. Dan stared into the eyes of the statue, wishing that it would spring to life. That Jesus would walk right off the cross and save him, but he knew that wouldn't happen. He had learned his whole life that God rarely made an appearance and that bad things happened to good people.

"Good people," Dan said it out loud without realizing it. The door to the confessional blew outward, flying across the church, breaking the crucifix in half. Lucifer's hand that gripped the side of the confessional was no longer human, clawed and massive, at least twice the size of a man's. He rounded the corner, revealing his massive frame. Dan was struck with terror at the sight before him. Red sigils pulsed along his arms and chest. His face, which was once young and beautiful, now looked old and scarred. Rows of razor-sharp fangs lined his wide carnivorous smile. The nose and eyes were absent, covered by a thick plate of white bone. Atop his head was a crown made of fire.

"Dear God," Dan mumbled as the large hand grasped him around the throat, tossing him through the old wood, spilling him out onto the church floor like a rag doll. Alarm bells were going off in Dan's entire body as pain fired through him with each movement he made.

"You pathetic fucking mouse," Lucifer said with disappointment dripping from the words. "I am going home, Dan. I will build a ladder out of the bones of everyone you have ever talked to if I have to."

Dan lifted himself up, resting his hip against one of the broken pews. "You keep saying how terrible we are." Dan's breath felt raspy, like a rib had hit something important inside. He tried to block out the pain as Lucifer stomped forward, shaking the very foundation of the old church.

The pain sent waves of nausea through his whole body, but Dan forced the words through gritted teeth. "What about your kind?" he yelled, trying to take the pressure off his chest by grabbing the massive hand. "You keep saying how we don't deserve this planet. That we shit on everything and everyone and you're right. We are horrible."

"Then absolve me and take responsibility!" Lucifer tightened his grasp, lifting Dan even higher.

"We are born weak, crying for anything to comfort us and we never stop. We ruined this oasis that we were given. We lie, we cheat, we tell God it's his fault, and then we cry when we think he's abandoned us. We think we're owed his love and protection, that we don't need to earn it. We think we're perfect but we're not built that way. We were never meant to be perfect."

Lucifer gripped his other hand around Dan's side, crunching through his bottom two ribs.

"Time is running out. I've told you this all night. I've proven to you that you're all miserable, ungrateful things. I don't need to hear you babble until you bleed out. Acknowledge my confession and take responsibility for my fall!"

Dan's consciousness was fading. His wounds made his entire body spasm in pain. Dan fought to stay awake. He thought of Max and clung to the hope that he could see them again one day, wherever he was going after this.

"No!" he spit the words, leaving a trail of bloody saliva connecting him and Lucifer like some unholy umbilical cord.

Dan was soaring through the air. Time seemed to slow as he passed over the broken wood that had once been the confessional. Dan smiled, hopeful that the impact would finally kill him as he collided with the wall. He felt a snap and his legs went cold, but to his dismay, he was still breathing. He prayed God would help him, somehow intervene, or at least to let him die. His prayers were interrupted by a hand yanking his head back, bringing him face to face once more with Lucifer.

"Why?"

It was a question they both needed an answer to. He lifted Dan up by the throat once more, spreading his scarred and broken wings behind him. Tears began to run down Dan's cheeks. From terror, from beauty, and from things Dan couldn't describe in that moment.

"Because I was born selfish, lustful, ignorant and wrathful, but I choose to be better. Every day I try to be better. You were born perfect, the literal light, and all you could see were the flaws in us. You chose to be worse. That's the difference between you and me. Between humanity and you. That's why we are his favorite. Our flaws give us a choice. That's what Joshua understood about us. *That's* why he chose us over you."

Dan's jaw dislocated from the impact when the back of Lucifer's hand connected with his face with a loud smack. The force drove his body down, breaking the floor on impact. Lucifer stood over him, his form seeming to stretch into a mass of shadow, filling the church with flame and darkness. Dan rolled his head, trying to catch his bearings, when he came face to face with the broken crucifix. The Christ's eyes seemed to be looking into Dan's soul, telling him it would all be over soon, all he had to do was hold on a little longer. Dan placed his hand gently on the cheek of the statue, leaving a bloody handprint across its face. He knew the blow would come any minute now, some giant foot stomping down on his skull or a fist hammering down, driving his bones into his organs. He didn't care, he just wanted it to be over. He was lifted into the air again, this time by the back of his hair.

"Look at me."

Dan didn't break eye contact with the statue.

"I said look at me!" Lucifer roared, finally getting Dan's attention.

Their eyes met, Lucifer's full of rage, Dan's full of contentment.

"He would be disappointed in you," Dan said, casting his glance down at the statue. Lucifer's eyes drifted towards the image of Joshua. It disturbed him. Joshua—tortured for eternity in stone. He looked at Dan, his broken and battered frame covered in blood. The image brought back thoughts to the day they had beaten and killed Joshua and how helpless he had felt. The same helpless feeling he felt now.

"Nobody sees you because..."

He released his grasp, dropping Dan's body hard amongst the broken wood, like a child who was done with a toy. He turned, spreading his wings and driving them down, picking up speed until he hovered off the ground. He looked back over his shoulder, glancing from the statue to Dan and then launched himself through the roof of the church. Dan collapsed on the floor, his body finally giving in to exhaustion.

↓ ↓ ↓ ↓ ↓ ↓

Dan was shaken awake by the rattle of the gurney as it was lifted down step by step.

"Hey, he's awake."

The paramedics made sure the cart was stable before one flashed a light into Dan's eyes.

"You ok there, padre?"

Dan's pupils adjusted to the flash, his vision finally clearing as the young man's face came into view.

"What happened to the church? Who attacked you?"

On the rooftop, Dan saw a giant bat-like wing shuffle out of view.

"There! Up there!" he shouted, pointing.

The paramedic looked, shining his flashlight up at the empty rooftop.

"Who?"

"The Devil! It's the Devil, damnit!"

Dan started shifting in his seat. The man tried calming him down, but it only made him more agitated as he slapped the man's hands away.

"Ok, ok, bud."

"I'm telling you the Devil is real damnit. He's here. He wanted me to forgive him."

The two men grasped Dan's arms, holding him in place.

"Let me go, damnit! I need to find my family!"

Dan didn't even feel the needle until it was too late. The warmth crept through his body, trapping him. A prisoner in a cage made of skin and bone. The two men collected themselves, lighting up cigarettes as they headed toward the front of the ambulance to finish their paperwork.

Dan tried to tell them. He tried to warn them of the nightmare making its way toward them even as his eyelids grew heavy, even as he was losing consciousness.

He tried to draw their attention to the clawed hand as it neared his throat.

The hand stopped and placed the tiny skull of a mouse on Dan's chest as he faded into the darkness.

Patreon Thanks

To my wonderful Patreon subscribers—your support allows me to write and drink copious amounts of espresso.

A huge thank you to
- Kristine Prais
- Kimberley Kraft
- Xelha Lopez
- Rosie Will
- Alexandra Russell
- Angie Valentine
- Becca Rogers
- Andrea Johnson
- Shannon O'Neil

This book would not be possible without you.

Also by Matthew Lutton

10 Drink Minimum

Candy Dish

In our Tears, In the Sea

Featured In:

Netipotcalypse: A Collaborative Novel

Seasons of Fear: Horrors for Every Holiday

About the author

Matthew Lutton is an up-and-coming author who currently haunts Marysville, Washington. Originally growing up in a sunny beach town in California, Matthew's imagination was sparked by the eerie and unexplainable happenings that would occur in the quiet corners of the city. He has always been fascinated with the horror genre, and began writing his own stories as a way to explore his dark and twisted thoughts.

Matthew's debut book, "10 Drink Minimum" delved deep into the darkness of the human soul, exploring themes like fear, desperation, and madness. His tales are a unique blend of psychological horror, supernatural mystique, and visceral violence. Each story is crafted with precision, creating a world that is both hauntingly realistic and unforgettably surreal. His second book, "Candy Dish" gives the reader sinfully delicious tales reminiscent of Tales from the Crypt, the Twilight Zone and Black Mirror.

Matthew's works are listed on Amazon.com and he runs a Patreon which can be found at www.patreon.com/mattluttonauthor

Printed in Dunstable, United Kingdom